Dog on Fire

FLYOVER FICTION *Series editor: Ron Hansen*

University of Nebraska Press Lincoln

It is my pleasure to thank Gay Walley and Sheila Kohler, Floyd Memorial Library, Yaddo, the MacDowell Colony, the hardworking UNP staff, and of course Steve Bull.

Chapters 1, 2, 4, 6, and 8 published as "My Brother's Dust" in *Conjunctions* 51, the Death issue, Fall 2008.

Chapter 12 published as "Electricity" in *Columbia*, Issue 26, Spring 1996.

Chapter 26 published as "Halloween Hunt" in *Flights*, September 2005.

The University of Nebraska Press is part of a land-grant institution with campuses and programs on the past, present, and future homelands of the Pawnee, Ponca, Otoe-Missouria, Omaha, Dakota, Lakota, Kaw, Cheyenne, and Arapaho Peoples, as well as those of the relocated Ho-Chunk, Sac and Fox, and Iowa Peoples.

∞

Library of Congress Cataloging-in-Publication Data
Names: Svoboda, Terese, author.
Title: Dog on fire / Terese Svoboda.
Description: Lincoln: University of Nebraska Press, [2023] | Series: Flyover fiction
Identifiers: LCCN 2022034866
ISBN 9781496235169 (paperback)
ISBN 9781496235879 (epub)
ISBN 9781496235886 (pdf)
Subjects: BISAC: FICTION / Literary | LCGFT: Novels.
Classification: LCC PS3569.V6 D64 2023 |
DDC 813/.54—dc23/eng/20220722
LC record available at https://lccn.loc.gov/2022034866

Set in Minion Pro by L. Auten.

For Paul

One fire burns out another's burning

—Shakespeare, *Romeo and Juliet*

Dog on Fire

one

1

Out of a storm so thick with dust, a storm so charged with first-rate prelightning ions that the grit flashes and the car dials fade, a storm so dark no taillight shines through, though drivers have flicked on every emergency switch, out of a storm even this dust bowl state stops for, I spot my brother with a shovel.

Men who shovel look alike. They all face where the wood joins the metal or at least their glance grazes there on its way to the shovel tip, so all you see is head or hat—in this case, a cap brim, most likely lettered *Feed and Seed* if I know my brother, tilted at some unreadable angle. What I can read while I creep the car forward, seeing and not seeing, is that he is not about to dig, he has dug; his shovel is now raised up. What he has dug swirls around us—me, in my car creeping through all this flying grit, and him, seen just in the time it takes to see, where lightning now laves and leaves.

Don't stop, moans the semi behind me, hauling cattle or, empty, having hauled. Don't pull over, says the dust smacking the car.

How do I know it's him I've seen? Only my brother would dig beside the road in this dust, because he is a digger. Besides, the road's right next to my father's land, and along its perimeter my brother would dig in postholes for the fences that fall over in the shrinkage of winter or sag with the swell of summer. Or else he could be digging to cover up something. Or maybe he was digging just for the hell of it.

I guess that last is what he is doing, with emphasis on *hell*. Just the way our cousin in another state was caught outside her parked vehicle, holding up her unwrapped baby to a tornado—was caught more than once—my brother has always dug too deep.

The glimpse goes, is gone. But even if I pull over and park here to check it out—which I should anyway, given that I can't see a damn thing and can hear only this semi shortcutting its own way behind me, honking now and then like a boat lost in fog, the sound a semi that could wallop right into me would make if it were too close—even if I do stop and park and get out and walk over to the field where he must be, he will not be there. He's dead.

I tap on my brakes. I make the tapping lively, not nervous, as I go along so slowly—it's really an SOS, not a signal to my brother behind me. I push my window button again just to hear my windows roll their clinch even tighter. I don't want to breathe his dirt in, all that grit that could be his. We're already close, too close, eleven months, one foot in the womb, the other in the—

I tap it out.

If I could Morse code him with these taps, it would be: *I'm not stopping now, the way I never stopped for you before*. But there can be no *ifs* to think about with the foghorn of the semi rattling my car. Or is that sound something else? Some other moan? Some way I bypass him that is deeper, that I can't get around at all or hear right?

The dust everywhere is so charged that the radio's gone static. This charge is my brother's fault too, a charge he gives off even when he's behind me and dead, being someone with too much electricity in his head that will forever discharge. He had spells. All that electricity from his *petit* and *grand mal* is probably still around here—so much of it, it probably killed him. If that isn't enough, he even attracted electricity, the raw kind that cooks. It will cook me too, its bits of lightning zapping through the dust like white knives. Or are those sparks because I have come to where the meteor landed a hundred feet off, that break it makes in my father's land that's a giant pock all alive, all glittery with electricity, its dirt dancing up and down on the radio waves and having a day?

The land here, if it is land I'm on and not road, is as flat as the road. I am leaning into the wheel and my arms ache trying to lean it straight. The roads around here are flat and straight. If I'm off the road, then that meteor hole is around here somewhere for sure and I will fall into it. I glimpse my father's crew cut pasture through the dust—that is, the crew cut that should *sh-sh* my car's underside if I'm driving on the pasture, the crew cut that disappears in another woof of dust into where I think might be the meteor hole—but then all that dust shimmies up again and takes over. No *sh-sh*.

At least the semi still calls behind me. As long as I can hear it, I know I'm on the road and not where my brother stands, so to speak, in my father's field. All of what's swirling is my brother's dirt now—I'm sure it is—his disturbance, his unquiet, his dug dirt whipping up the storm's storm. The semi calls again, and this time real lightning answers it, about the fanciest electricity yet, a tree of it not three feet from my hood, hot and white at the end of the pasture.

Where I once again see him.

He's in the same position as before. But I don't really expect him to be posed any different—he's dead, after all. It's me who should be moving. Or do I just circle him with all my straight driving? His mouth is open. What's he trying to say? *The dust the dust the dust*—he's there forever, trying to be heard. Then he's gone.

I turn on the AC, because of sweat, the kind that comes when all the windows are up, and so is fear. What am I afraid of? That he will take his revenge for every time I turned away from him? That what he was saying is that I will get what I deserve?

I need my phone, its blank face to sweat into, some nonsense talk to take place outside of this dust- and lightning-blinded shortcut, the solace of company or fear shared, and not just this silly moaning semi that's obviously more lost than me, that has obviously driven way off the road and is hoping to make its way back via some answering moan before it hits the meteor hole—that is, if the driver knows about the hole and doesn't think that land is only flat and straight with no lessons to be learned.

There are lessons to be learned is what seeing him twice in the dust says to me.

I've left the phone at home.

Sweat runs into the lifelines of my palms where the dirt collects, where I grip the wheel's plastic. His lifelines are dust, I think, that kind of dirt. I flex my gritty palms. Forget about lifelines—I just want to push down on the pedal and arrive. My workplace isn't that far, just a few miles, at least when I started shortcutting down this road. If I accelerate now, I'll be there, I'll be out of this brother-ridden storm. But before I put on the gas, I honk as if my brother will hear me and clear away. I honk back at the semi, but there's no more moaning.

That's not good.

A battered blue Chevy passes me—where did that come from?—with some poor dirt farmer hunched over the wheel, not my brother. I stare into the dull screen of my side mirror and back at the road, I stare and I stare. Then the semi finally passes me, one wheel at a time, with a *thank god* honk that shakes my car, the dirt swirling over and around us.

I never think my brother might want to see me.

2

When I park, I am still shaking from my trip through the dust, though the storm has passed with big fat drops and a curtain of rain. I shake myself calm, then I get out of the car and cross the lot to the grain elevator to pick up my son.

Today my wee fifteen-year-old has squeezed his six-one frame into the elevator's afterthought office, trailer-squat and fiercely air-conditioned, to tend my screen after the archiving of my workday, a summer job I made up for any adolescent, but one I filled with him. I help out at the grain elevator for money. Alone most of the time, I track sales, register the loads, pay the slips, and get the phone when it needs getting. It's a good job for what they call a grass widow around here, somebody whose husband has slid back into the grass and down the lousy hole he came out of, the preferred hell of the ex. I left home for that husband and came back years lighter, my mothering career almost over, my wifing best forgotten, and a humanities degree that made me human and jobless. I help out at the elevator sometimes seven days a week, when there's lots of grain to be shipped or stored.

Something has interfered with my screen that my son has to fix. A kernel of corn? Wheat?

My son laughs as if I've guessed it, then points toward the ladies'.

Aphra glides out of the bathroom on feet too small to bear her three hundred pounds, especially in the breast area. She gives me a nod and takes a seat with a *whump*. She could be in the process of lightening up by two hundred pounds, given the copious sweat she exudes. Wet hair barely holds to her skull in twisted sprays, another way she tries to spread herself around. Even her clothes reach. They pull out of where they are tucked; they exhale around her body in a nimbus of cloth both too tight and too loose, in colors that plaid their way into confusion. She says I have to help her first, says my son, in a not-too-quiet whisper. It's like I'm her tech guy.

You do have a reputation, I say.

He doesn't shrug so much as repel my presence, my being in the room. But I am at least a shield.

My drive? Aphra holds up her device to be fixed. The tone of her voice insinuates: *You broke it.* The tone also commands: *Fix it, or I'll run my nail across a blackboard.* The fat on her arm waves in recoil to the item being suspended. Not enough of a disheveled half sleeve hides the arm's bareness—and strength. She could snap that thumb drive in two with a finger is what her bulk suggests.

My dead brother learned what he learned about girls from Aphra, and not without protest. Twenty years earlier she circled our place during his time at high school, yelling plaintive *Okays?* She threw her shoes at our door, with an even more coquettish *Please?* She wasn't even in high school anymore, so it was a parody *Please* to everyone else. Every male of any age in our small town of high school track-star cops and crooks had taken time with her in the dark, where one noticed less the harsh arrangement of her features and the limbs so generously pillowed. My brother, while being not as comely as said track stars but of soft heart, made the mistake of giving a kindly *Thank you* to her *Please.*

My son holds up his hand to her. Not yet.

Some storm that was, I say to her. I don't say my brother was in it. No, I would never say that—I would never mention him to her, ever. That would make her sad, and her sadness, I fear, would overwhelm me like everything else about her overwhelms. I have not seen her since the service for him a month ago, but I never know when I'll see her next. She makes beds, now and then, for a motel that verges on having no beds to be made, so her appearances are never to be predicted. Especially now that my brother is gone.

I take an air-conditioned cold folding chair and wait for my son to finish.

Did you know that Aphra means dust in Hebrew? I love all that dust, she says. It reminds me of your brother.

She, on the other hand, has the right to talk about him, to bring him up. After all, she found my brother first, nude and dead and not a mark on him. Maybe he shouted for help and she heard him. Maybe she was there all the time. She was unclear and distraught and evasive after.

It was very dusty, I say.

Church bells start ringing. The elevator is just far enough from town that their evening Angelus, though faint, obscures whatever she says next. They ring every day at the afterwork hour, six, when you think *God help me with dinner*. It's my brother's bell that's ringing, among others. My grandmother bought church bells for the family males, only the males. She wanted a secure slot for her post-peasant descendants, good farmers, good lawyers, doctors—or even just a good male nurse—and what better way to start than from above, with a clapper? The sex of these bells stopped swinging when their innards were remade with a recording that plays its tunes by remote control, but they still release the proper male peals on time for God's six o'clock notice.

I have bell envy.

He ascended, she repeats.

Ascended? I say. I know who *he* is.

The Ascension, like the Virgin's. She leans toward me, her breasts rippling like loose muscles in her scoop neck. Remember Charlton Heston in a white robe and sandals? The bells reminded me.

You don't think he's buried?

I went to check on him three days after, she says.

And? I brush the dust off my shirt—his dust?

My legs went light, she says. It was like he wanted me to join him. She turns her eyes up to where heaven should be, according to those who believe up is the location.

I noticed somebody's footprints where the sod was soft, I say, when I collected the vases.

They would've been his prints, she snaps. I would never walk on the actual fresh laid grave.

Her eyes, set deep in the plump rolls of her face, take me in all at once, as if just noticing me. It's a hard thing to return that kind of stare. Of course, he's not Jesus, she says, as if I haven't figured that out.

I make a nervous laugh. I'll bet they had a beer up there, waiting for my brother. No, wait—wine. That's what they drink.

He never liked wine.

Right, I say. It upsets me that she knows what he likes—a little. Of course she knows. They ended up close.

I remember when my brother tried to shake Aphra by walking to school instead of driving, a setup more embarrassing to a teenager than being greeted by a sibling in study hall. He would hide in a crabby widow's spiked bushes and sprint through backyards patrolled by craven dogs on long chains. He was not saving himself for a prom queen or even Ivy Jones, the girl with the pointy red glasses, the one Aphra suspected, but saving himself in the more literal sense.

I decide she smothered him to death.

He would have had to suck air between breasts in any act done to completion. She did find him nude in the kitchen, a place where food and sex might intersect. But the premeditated seems to lie outside her circle of meditation. She is of the minute. This hunger of hers blankets all sense of time, fully obliterating the deliberate. Already she is opening a snack, its bag so small as to seem part of the snack, wrenching the pressed-together bits of cellophane apart with her worn teeth. Always polite, she offers me the first dive, she shakes the bag so I know I have to take one, a big *Or Else* at the other end of her shake. Or is this my prejudice against the weight-challenged? She radiates a toxic you-can-catch-this-from-me anger. It could be grief. My anger is with my brother for having died where she could find him. I don't want her chip. To take her chip and eat it would be sharing grief.

She chews down a chip from the bag that she's freed. They're cheese-sprayed, she explains, swallowing, then smiling, showing their orange between teeth that need work.

I eat the next chip and wonder how long my son will take with my tech problem, and how long with hers. He's so intent on the screen that I suspect it's a game he's fixing instead. Then I imagine Aphra undressed. Then I imagine a book, some kind of operating manual for women, the kind with charts that you are led to believe correspond. I can see my brother leafing through it, one hand searching for the parts as if in the dark of a tool chest, the other pressing the paperback open, breaking its back.

Ascension is much like sex, I decide. You're allowed your own body while you ascend, pant by pant, and surely the release is the release the sun and you feel from touching so close. Then birds towing welcome ribbons rush over to cover your nakedness, all that body. Then maybe you drink the wine.

I stay quiet, though. I don't tell her what I think.

She finishes her bag, wads it into a lump that springs back into shape as soon as it misses the basket. She creases her mouth forlornly.

Why do I dislike her so much? Do I think by keeping my brother in thrall, she put a stop to the life he could have lived, working at something more lucrative or at least less hard-on-his-back work? I was all the mother he had, because our mother wasn't as involved as a mother should be, and maybe the possessive or ambitious questions come up when any new woman comes on the scene in that setup?

My son is slowly tapping at the computer keys. I sidle over to check his screen. He's on my job. He's not really so slow; he is just hoping Aphra will move on, that whatever she needs she will find somewhere else. Cosmically, he whispers.

Comically, I say and gesture toward the file cabinet. I pull out the top drawer, and we confer behind it. A sense of humor is all you need, I say. We have to be nice. Remember, she dogs you only because you look like him.

He shrugs. All my life? I have to look like him every day? He can barely get out the words, he is so angry.

Aphra hoists herself to her feet, wields her broken drive closer, unpockets the second piece of it.

My son stays reasonable. No, he can't repair that kind of damage, which perhaps she herself inflicted so she could lie in wait for him.

He doesn't whisper.

She titters and drops the drive bits into the basket that she missed with the chip bag, then she steps closer. That's too bad, she says. Her big smile flashes its orange. She looks as if she could swallow him whole. Instead, she clears phlegm from somewhere. Say, she says, could you please move a little to the left?

My son pretends my tidying the desk makes it too noisy to hear her.

She wants him to move in front of the AC, and she has it in her to insist. Genes, or chemistry under the sway of genes, must force her. She moves fast and leans toward him. It is only a small, small thing, you understand—smell, your uncle's smell. Her voice drops in sadness.

There isn't room to wedge myself between them. My son shudders.

Near enough, she inhales deep and long. She is not greedy, inhaling over and over. She steps back, and I worry that she will trip, turning away, she lumbers so, and then maybe fall. Once the fire department had to come, Joe Broward and the other big guy, the only ones who can lever her back to standing without compromising themselves, without her sniffing at them, too, as if she were some kind of bear, heat-struck and lonely.

She teeters.

I would be the one to telephone those volunteers.

3

That chip bag was mostly crumbs and salt anyway. I have six more inside Sport, parked pretty close. His sister liked her chip, I know she did. It would kill her to say so. They like to laugh at me, his sister and her son. You would think by now I wouldn't care, that Ha, ha, ha is just spit now.

I am filled with the perfume of him, like gas in a balloon that floats.

Okay, Sport, let's go. I don't care where. So perky, Sport is like having a whole different body, with a rabbit's get-up-and-go. Her brother paid the last payment not a month before he died.

I can say "he died" to myself now. I don't know about out loud. We were so in love. In joy, I like to say, and I am no girl to give her heart away easy. Her brother was not the only guy on the block, and he knew it. One guy actually got up, put on his boots, and left ten dollars on the nightstand. Before it even started to be dawn! It was a two-way insult, that he should pay, and that amount. The problem was, I saw the guy the very next day at the Dairy Queen where I used to clean up. I told him when I got him in the back room that I was pregnant. I didn't really know, and he gave me real money, five hundred dollars. Even after it turned out I wasn't, I didn't give it back. How could he find out what the test said in the end? I am mean like that. After my dad, I didn't care.

Her brother gave me a rose one time. It was wrapped in real tissue but droopy. It had been sitting in his car awhile. That was my fault, because I had him wait so long—making a man wait is what they do on TV for maximum effect—while I decided on the chartreuse sweater. I had to look all around to find the leggings that matched. I had that rose on top of my bureau for two months in a vase with water and an aspirin to perk it up. After that, I shut it up in a dictionary and put his big Shakespeare on top. That pressed the petals good and flat so I could keep them forever. However long that is I don't want to know.

4

I eat like this so Aphra won't come after me, says my son. He wields his spoon in his mouth as if he is some kind of weirdo, the bowl of it upside down and himself draped, as only adolescents drape, stomach-first over a mostly flattened ottoman on wheels he's rolled into my father's kitchen.

I blow my still dirt-filled nose.

He scoops at the air with his spoon, then flips to his back and propels the furniture crab-like along one wall, spoon out. Sir Real, he says, very carefully. How we had to use the side panel of your computer to get Aphra up. Get it—Mr. Real?

I agree. Definitely surreal levering her up off the floor. You're a genius to think of it, I say. Thank god I didn't have to call the fire department.

My son grunts and begins to do sit-ups with the ottoman for balance, his legs hooked impossibly over the side.

Even as a teenager, my brother didn't do things like that. The electricity in his head might go off. It went off in stores and parking lots and museums and at communion rails and in front of any best friend. He took medicines for it that were never right, that changed him into someone else, more mean than not. As a kid, he would corner me in a room and Indian burn me, punch me in the stomach, and laugh. I clawed and bit back and got punished—*Look at that scar!*—but he was never caught with a mark. And if he were caught, well, he had spells. Did he have those spells in front of everyone to spite me, the spiteful? After the spells, he was different. So sweet.

I shower and scrub at the dirt, but the dirt grit is everywhere. Eyelid grit, towel grit, toe grit, grit between my teeth, kiss grit.

I don't say kiss grit to my son when I come out of the shower. Kissing isn't something you discuss with someone as old as he is. VD you could discuss, or even more likely AIDS, something they discuss so thoroughly in class. Kissing is too personal, something that they learn outside of class that they could be seen learning.

My son is already working his spoon over a second large mound of Chex cereal in a bowl, his stopgap snack. I insert frozen dinner things into the oven. While my son eats, he exudes charm. By this, I mean he takes a sudden interest in my money, an interest he began to make clear during our drive home from the elevator a mere hour earlier, wanting the purchase of a cord or a widget or more ROM for his computer.

The specific charm he exudes consists of watching me while he discusses this interest. Boys his age ordinarily regard their mothers without regard or discussion, so watching me is charming. I know I am doing nothing a boy would find watchable. I am not lighting a match to interest wannabe pyromaniacs, nor inspecting my bra; I am returning to the chore of throwing away the coupons my brother collected and my father gave me to sort, he not having the interest in my theories about how my brother died that I do. I am throwing them out by date of expiration the way my father can't—the print is too fine—because that last date might tell me something.

My brother's body across the clean kitchen floor.

I am not the one to wonder, to pick, and to pry. I can watch a big bird settle on a dusty leaf and not crane or open a window to crane. But my brother was way too close to me in age and, of course, with his dying for no reason, really much too close not to wonder.

What else is there to do here other than wonder? There are bake sales, gossip, a football pool, and school games—and the ricochet of absent living. Moving away from a divorce is good, but it will leave a void of friends and places. I had become used to seeing the snow that high or a swamp out back, not the usual old cottonwood trees rattling, and the swirls of dust. Even though this is where I grew up, there's change here too: someone not neglecting their yard, a new motor home, a remodeled church deluxe—lots of room for ricochet and pattern.

He took new medicines for his spells: clobazam, lorazepam, sertraline, and more.

I'll have to think about whether we can afford whatever else you need, I tell my son. Was it memory you wanted?

Ha, he says, you've got too much of that.

He's right of course. What I really can't forget is that while my brother was dying, he must have tried hard to call—the receiver had fallen off its cradle. Or else it was Aphra not putting it back. He didn't have a cell phone. Those who came to get him found him easily, his house being in town, but not too quickly. They were in the midst of wrapping holiday presents for the festivities that were soon to come, and carving last-minute initials into things that couldn't be wrapped, when the *ooga* sounded. Time opens up in an emergency anyway—it makes a wedge between would-be rescuers and the would-be rescued where the rules don't matter.

My father noticed the receiver off the cradle later.

My father enters, and like my son, he, too, is struck by a sudden hunger. It is his house we have been living in since I moved back with my grass-widow status, a status my brother could never claim and one my father finds handy these days in the housekeeping department, since my mother is on a long, long vacation from her scotch. He pours out the few Chex left, the frozen food still being, for the most part, frozen. The dust storm he only saw through a window, office-bound as he was this afternoon, struggling with a bank officer over a tithing arrangement for his French sunflower crop, an arrangement he says now is as inaccessible as a calendar girl. At least there wasn't hail behind the dust, he sighs, hearing of Aphra and her drive, my son's lack of money, and then about my brother turning up at the shortcut so close to his land, although I say *I thought I saw*.

My son says I better get glasses.

I don't remember your brother the way you do, my father says between bites. He made a good banana bread. Before your mother left, she gave his crockpot to the poor.

It's only been what? A month? I put aside the coupons and chew on a couple of squares of cereal that missed my father's bowl. My son chews louder, and then says it's like Hamlet and my brother's the ghost. He wants revenge.

He gives us his best soliloquy.

So just who do you think I saw? I ask over all this chewing and acting.

It could've been my hired hand, my father says. He's not that much shorter than your brother was.

I know what he looks like.

A ghost, says my son. The play within the play that reveals all, he says, giving me his best profile. We studied it: the sword through the curtain, that blood-soaked curtain. He stabs with his spoon.

Finish your food, I say.

The ruined curtain, says my son anyway, pointing to a spot on the wall beside our food and burping.

My father laughs.

My son goes back to watching me, and eating. My brother would chew that loud and watch, and then I'd find gum stuck to the inside of my bowl or a fake thumb in the milk. I move slowly even now, under such a watching. Dinner in five minutes, I say, as if he's extracted a confession.

Did Great-Uncle Beck actually invent Jell-O? my son asks, bringing his bowl to the sink.

Yes, says my father.

He did not claim that often, I say. I mean he sometimes did say something like that, but as to the actually—I don't think so. Or somebody else held the patent on it, or else nobody could hold it, because ladies all over the world already knew about it. Your uncle, however, had his own Jell-O ideas.

My father approves of my speech with a shake of his head.

I know, I know, sighs my son, against the tedium of familial recitation. Only two people bought his Jell-O cushion: the high school teacher who planned to use it as a seat for his hemorrhoids, whose wife threw it out, and the lady with the old dog that liked the taste of it.

My son takes a long drink of milk straight from the carton.

Don't, I say, automatically.

While swallowing, he gets that sad look of knowing he's done wrong. Then he gasps: How could your brother have good ideas? He lived around here.

You need more pavement for good ideas? asks my father. More trouble and people to dish it out to? A lot of rooms full of pictures painted by the dead with their troubles on their brushes and graffiti on the buildings to boot? A city? He tilts his chin up to make his point in the negative.

Jeez, gramps.

He's probably right is the long and short of it, I say. Your uncle did live away from home for a while, like you will.

I will, Mom. I'll move closer to where they make the milk.

He offers me the carton. I look inside it as if he has slipped between its lips and drowned or as if he will step out of the bottom, all grown. Of course it's empty. He's all smiles, having tricked me into the disposing of it. Ha, he says and begins singing "Home, Home on the Deranged," and my father knows even better words than he does.

I serve what I've warmed, just a sniff underdone, the center of the entrée a bit crunchy with ice crystals. No one complains, just as no one volunteers to go out into the dark and fetch more milk at the store on the corner, nor do the dishes.

Tonight I open the window over the sink. The night is bare of stars, the late summer petering out with who-knows-what dust or rain weather, the kind that wears out the warmer days in clouds. Nothing to look at, except in memory.

My brother did leave here, but he went not that far away. He was trying not to farm but to struggle, like all sons, for a place in the world without his father. He found a town with a company that hired him to shovel in trenches and pick up extra boards from sites that weren't quite built yet. People would come at night with pickups to steal these boards if he didn't stow them. He did his work after the site was closed and fit the boards behind cable or Sheetrock in the lockup. Who knows how many of those boards you have to pick up in a place like that in order to keep visiting the grocer's, to pay for Tylenol, to stand in a mall now and then and ask directions? He was as thin as a board after.

Maybe he dug a little between picking up boards. He was always digging.

Where he had gone to live must have been like here, or anywhere else where they have those building sites, where you don't know why all the stores close at three on the first Monday of the month, why the pastor drives a cut-down Chrysler, why the cinnamon buns unwind backward, or the water tastes like ash.

Afterward, my father said he should come back and at least try to farm. My brother listened, and brought back mystery. Before he left, there was nothing outside of where he went during his spells that he could tell us about without us already knowing. There was so much he did not tell us after he returned.

They had birds there, he said when my father bought the garage like a house for my brother and he moved in.

Birds? my father asked.

He meant birds you could buy, not that he bought one, those birds in cages built out of thin boards, slats really, to keep the birds in. An old lady sold them. These birds were not strong enough to break out of their cages, he said. They beat their wings against those slats.

Birds? we repeated.

He came back because those birds reminded him of the birds in cages that can't breathe at the bottom of a mine.

My son returns and dries the dishes. I'm suspicious.

When the last dish is stored, my son says, Can I count up how much is in the creamer? Aha! I applaud his dishes-for-cash approach, and the creamer hasn't been subject to probate. At my least signal *Go*, he starts digging into my brother's creamer, one cast in the shape of a bronco. My brother did not like him fooling with this creamer, and probably this is his change that still fills it. My brother also did not like him looking so much like him year after year. I think he thought it wiped out the mystery he had gained. For example, where was that creamer from? Not from Las Vegas, which is stamped on its bottom, according to my brother. Years ago, visiting, my son would guess anywhere else over and over, and my brother didn't like that either. My son's flaw was he didn't have spells.

My son scatters the coins across the table, picks out the quarters, and jams the rest back in. Take the pennies too, says my father from behind his paper, but he doesn't bother.

The creamer was last fully emptied when my brother was ten years or so older than my son is now and back from the town he went off to. With these pennies and car wash money, movie-candy-saved money, and gambling profits—Will this fluff fall first for a quarter?—my brother bought himself a car, a seriously dull cheap car that he paid for in full and then crashed just a year later in a spell. Then he had to be driven around, because they took so many points off for what my father decided had better be called speed instead of a spell. Before this crash, my brother invented the Jell-O cushion. After his crash, he was working on Jell-O-as-airbag. Who was ready for either?

Boys are always ready. I hand my son a bill of my own and tell him to buy milk at the corner, and bring home the change. I see him pocket the bill and smile, the way a boy would.

5

Her brother left me not six weeks after we got together the first time. He went somewhere else, another town entirely. I cried my eyes out after. It wasn't my fault he walked in on me with that cute guy from the fairgrounds. I was trying to show her brother how much I wanted him by seeing someone else. Seeing? he said, That was not seeing. He didn't understand that I couldn't get the time of day any other way. I wanted him to take a stand, then he did.

When he got back, he said if I wouldn't move in, then how could we get together?

I thought about that. I said I was afraid to move in. That's the truth, I said. What I didn't tell him is why. I just couldn't. It was because I didn't want people to think he was as bad as me. After all, he had that family of his, so la-di-da. I shut my mouth—but not about everything. For example, instead of farming, he wanted to outdo his dad by inventing something to do with Jell-O. I said, You should have that Jell-O you're always talking about explode out of a bag for the car. You'd have Jell-O all over your front, I said. Maybe you could add a little whipped cream. He had the biggest grin on his face that I have ever seen on a grown man anywhere. Plus, I'm the one who suggested the slogan: Jell-O up or die!

Anyway, I read books a lot while he was gone, mostly the heavy Shakespeare one. He told me that's what the rest of the world reads to make them smart, and he just didn't get it. It's like a whole different language, he said. You need clues to figure out who's the sword carrier and even who dies. So I read the CliffsNotes first. He said that was cheating. I liked the donkey. The queens were a lot more into murder instead of true love. Not enough princesses. I sent him a letter about it, which I now have back.

Dear You:

Let the good times roll, as Shakespeare said, if I remember correctly. No one asked me about you going away, but then nobody knew we were together, did they? Like Shakespeare, you must've given them a good story. But the book you left by him is so-so. Sometimes he's way off in another century or the people are very busy going exeunt. It makes me sad that I left my clothes in my own closet while you were here, but I thought they would keep my posters company. Spice Girls and J-Pop. Besides, your closet smells like motor oil. No, I haven't even been to the fairgrounds at all, not even for the fair. Love love love.

He wasn't in that town for as long as they think.

I have to go to the movies tonight. I could stream one, but that reminds me of him, banging on the internet connection to make it work better. I always told him that hurts the computer. Computers are very delicate, I said. Somehow it always listened to him though, and the movies would go along for quite a while after. Now I sit in the balcony of the real theater, and the romance keeps going on like a punch in the face.

6

Graves are what founded our town over a hundred years ago, not a brand of tires or a confluence of water or an aneurysm of oil. Here graves shot up out of opportunity—too much speculating and people got shot, or too little opportunity, a lack of food. Pretty soon, people passing by started to think of this place as where to dig a grave and grieve. They started to save up their dead just to stop here and dig. After people started burying here whomever they had because someone else had buried here, people started to stay and bury more. After a while, people couldn't move, out of either so much mourning or so much need or both, since people were needed to haul lumber for what graves contain and the usual appurtenances, meaning not only the boxes but the crosses, too, the handles, and the fence. And of course, soon some professional was needed to hammer things together better than the others, and someone else was needed to sell the nails for that hammer and the coffee it took to get that hammering good and tight, and someone had to say something better than the others to keep the dead dead, and all of them needed wives who fed the mourners and soon needed a little something extra for the children.

I stop driving around and through the cemetery and turn in at the library instead. These days, TV is mostly about sex, and boring because I have none now and no prospects. At the library, I hope to find better distraction. But on the shelves, I find only fiction that dwells on the same. The classics reek of it, and the trashy novels are simply light in motivation, the paperbacks with their covers of men naked from belt buckle up confusing me. I despair of any evening activity to divert me from thinking about my brother, or at least my brother-in-a-dust-storm, until I come across this history of the town, although I am sure it will be just a boring recitation of begets and land deals and swindles.

No—graves. Wouldn't you know it.

Maybe people died here on purpose, just to get buried. Lots of towns must have had extra space for graves of people passing by. But here was a lot of digging, and the cemetery was soon packed, apropos of a city. The attraction has worn off lately, or fewer die all around or die here on purpose, because these days one backhoe does most of the work, whenever they need it. I don't know exactly what kind of custom digging my brother did along with farming for my father, but the digging he did was not often. The town didn't need more than one digger, at least not anymore, so he was alone.

He looked like someone who'd dug. Gray was his color, with a shine that rocks get a second after they're spit on. He was a rock that had been spit on—shiny enough but frozen good and gray in life, with the dates already cut into him. As regular in size as a stone in a row, with dark any-color eyes caught in a face that was always turning away—or yours was. Maybe I made up his goodness, maybe he never sent a card or called to congratulate me on my grass-widowhood. But he was the boy whose hand I held first, falling to the ground in a spell whenever and wherever, then forgetting me so easily, his eyes rolled up in white-out, babbling words like *pancake, where, if, president.* He usually didn't know who I was until after he recovered, at least not for a minute—like an hour if you're a kid. When he spoke after a spell, it was slow, a gradual drift onto what needed saying and then all at once too much of it, talk that ran on like a fear, into dark muttered corners and then silence. A spell.

Thanks, I tell the librarian. I'll take this history, and maybe some music. One of these instrumentals.

The library's not far from my father's house, but I would never walk, not these days. I like driving around better. I like being inside a car, where I can't be asked how I am by anyone, or squinted at with *Lovely day, isn't it?* It's been nearly a year since I moved here, but I'm still driving everywhere, no matter how small this place is. I like the driving part of grieving, its privacy. If that's what I'm doing.

On my way home there's the light.

The only one in town. Every time I stop, I think *Here's where Aphra pulled up next to me.* She always tried to be the one to drive my brother around after he lost his license. He had a bicycle, but he seldom rode it. That time I saw them together, it could have been some emergency, like a stitch at the hospital from a shovel-cut. I had just moved back. She mouthed, What are you doing here? and I did not answer her, although the light was two minutes long.

I couldn't answer her. I couldn't even return her look. I was shocked to see them sitting, one together with the other, in the front seat as if they were a number, as if they loved each other. After all, I was the one who had had a lover, who married him and begat offspring, all in the name of love, notwithstanding the final tally.

When he leaned past her toward me, it wasn't to see why I didn't answer or at least nod and wave. He was me, too—he wore my face of shame. I looked over to see it, and then the light changed and I drove off.

Why he didn't leap out of the car and into mine is the question. He was her captive is the answer. That was the kind of love they had, the caught kind, a webby one, where feelings no one would have thought unwound and stuck while the other kinds went on playing. I have had some experience with the caught kind that I had to leave so far behind as to come here and live with my father and help out at the elevator, caught so far as to compel a tearful divorce. So maybe it is my own shame, too, that shamed me, that I was so busy not looking or trying not to while Aphra talked to him at the light, speaking into his blank face so close, as if it were a microphone she used to make herself louder.

You can't die of shame. Shame might blaze up across the sky of your life, but you can't die of it.

Some say Aphra had something to do with the crash that caused him to need her to drive. I'm not saying who said that—of course Aphra brought on a spell and caused the car accident. Of course she loved to drive for him. Some say those emergencies he had happened on a schedule, and it wasn't his but hers.

Did he move away to that town, not to prove himself to his father, but to get away from Aphra, and then he returned to face that fear of her? That takes courage. When he came back from that other place, I heard that his face was pinched thin and brown. The brown part I had figured out: it wasn't that he was digging at night like some legend but that board picking up he must've done earlier, in the middle of the day, with no willow weeping that his usual place provided. It was the pinched part in his face I wondered over.

When my father or Aphra weren't driving him around, my brother used his bicycle, or he stayed home in the snow and rain and had the grocer deliver, a service so rare in our small town that it added to the caution of even the older children crossing his kicked-up yard. But there were still boys who shot BBs into his windows and laid dead cats on his doorstep and filled his yard with fill because they could. These boys hot-wired a truck full of fill to move it in front of his gate and let it dump. Not a hill of fill anymore but something of an incline right up to where you would think a walkway might start, or so my father said later. A lot of fill. Well, he couldn't shovel it off, could he? He had pride enough in his digging work, and a yard full of fill wasn't going to make him dig at home. The dirt blew, and the filled yard made him look even more like a Shove, which is what the boys called him. Hey, Shove, I heard them yell, Shove it.

These Shove-It boys were not my own boy's friends. He didn't have many friends yet, but these were not his. These boys tormented my brother when he was alive the way he tormented me, often and unthinking, but they had been known to torment others, and not just with dirt. All the sand bucketed out of the sandbox. Dead deer guts smeared across a driveway. A chicken pox of toothpaste dotting a picture window. Children crossing the park who turned up at the other side without money for a movie.

I think it was Aphra who scared these boys away from my brother's place, coming around as often as she did. It could have been. But despite all her scaring-away potential for my brother, he lived alone. So alone he lived, with junk mail in mounds as if it would be answered, the smell of boxed food, and a too-clean floor in a house the size of a garage with permanent garage stains on the walls, a house without so much as a crawl space. A house the size of a rocket ship, said my father when he was trying to sound up. After he bought it, he put in a stove and a fridge, then rented it to him.

It was my son, on a visit before we moved here, who guessed what my brother had hidden under a tarp around the side of his house. Aphra was in the picture then, but we didn't know how much, only enough to suspect her of being the source of this mystery, and didn't credit him. Even though the delivery van bore out-of-town plates and had the medallion of a washer maker painted on its side, it wasn't a washer. Too round and squat. Plenty of us guessed planter, but the why of that made us stupid with more guessing. Plants of that size? Him, a waterer? He laughed at us but didn't call us nosy idiots, nor did he confess. Up until the neighbors called the firemen to investigate the steam rising from under the tarp, my son's guess wasn't any more right than the others'.

It couldn't be that, not him. A hot tub?

No, I never knew what my brother was thinking. We weren't really close, except in age. Irish twins they used to call us, born less than a year apart. It didn't help to grow up with him, side by side. My brother was so close in age, I couldn't see him—he was my own hand in front of my face and probably vice versa. Maybe that's why he used to hit me. Not because he could, being stronger, but because he wanted that hand out of the way, or flailing with frustration at his condition, he wanted to make us evenly blind. I don't know why he dug. Why did he return to this town to do more of it? Why did he go in for a hot tub?

Why not?

I'm back in this town because there's room to park. I can leave the car two feet from the curb or at the wrong angle. No questions asked.

Except for Aphra. You have to hand it to her. She does want to know what I'm doing here.

7

His sister drives around like she's lost. It's the town she grew up in, for Chrissake, her whole family. Her son is like one slice of Wonderbread next to another with regard to his uncle. How much of her brother is still here, inside him, inside both her and him? And what about those parents? Him divided up. They had the money to set him up for a good life six times if they wanted to. Instead, they let him dig. Not that he ever complained. If they had helped him, were they afraid they would be setting me up too? I had nothing to do with his car crash, but I heard they think different. They doubted his spells would do that to him. They needed a different reason, one they could despise. I was never even at the wheel then.

That's the sort of thing I think about, with the movie going on, not the plot. They have to kill somebody pretty bad for me to really watch. And now that I know what dead looks like, I am not all that interested in the makeup. I practice being cold while I watch, and not thinking.

I asked his sister, when I seen her at the pharmacy picking up pep pills, how long is she staying? What is she doing here? I know that she once had a husband and he is not around. She probably has a life in another town, and friends there for sure. But if her husband died, I would have heard. Leaving everything behind sounds like divorce.

Scandal.

Not that that would make a bit of difference to me. I was getting change for my Pepto-Bismol, stuff that's perfect for after eating that spicy barbecue my mom likes, when I asked her what she was doing.

What does she answer?

The funeral seems like just yesterday, doesn't it? Then she snatches up her prescription as if it is going to dissolve in a puddle, like ice cream.

8

License plates lined the lot, enough cars with county numbers on their bumpers to make the funeral decent, which is what it was, enough people to sign several pages of the guestbook, names that certified a crowd had come to lay my brother to rest. The number also verified that he had a few friends, people we didn't know. Lining up that clutch of license plates beside the book, well, it seemed there must have been some names that weren't written in too, that had just had license plates we knew but couldn't place, or faces that stared back from people who came to funerals the way others went to yard sales where they didn't have so many graves. Or perhaps they read the paper that said sudden but natural death, and they thought, *What's natural at his age?* Even the real estate broker attended. A lot of people will come just to look at what the casket cradles, knowing full well how unnatural in general death is, over and over, whatever the cause. A stopped heart? Doesn't everyone get a stopped heart? Or maybe they came to shake their heads because of how few names in the end got written in the book, compared to someone else's book.

That's why Aphra made a fuss. She stood beside the book at the back and said no one should stay who hadn't signed in. She whispered it so loud in the direction of the family that we looked down as a family toward the casket, the only other area her large self did not yet occupy and command. Really, we were happy to have anyone come, so we ignored her and proceeded to view the casket, as directed.

On my turn, I peered in the way you do, with your eyes protruding as if to see all that's inside without moving your head any closer, but even that far away I could see it wasn't him, that the sinuses that had backed his eye bags and cheek ducts in allergy were drained and that his lips had come unpuffed from all the drugs he took for his spells. Without these disfigurements, his face was changed not so much into a sleeping stranger but into someone who could get up and start a new life incognito. I could tell it was him in the dust storm later, but in repose, who knew who the undertaker had made him into? He had a smile so smothered you couldn't be sure he wasn't frowning.

My father sobbed the entire time, in a sort of soggy shock, while my mother stood stern. She had her flask.

Everyone left for the cemetery, signed in or not.

Police with their hats off stopped the traffic when we met green lights on our slowed-down drive to the plot. This courtesy went for anybody dead in the town, maybe a throwback from when the dead were more of a business, but it surprised me. *Who cares about robbers or con artists or interstate speeders?* was what those hats off said, with a respect I hadn't suspected from that lot of ex-football ends, now policemen, who had a Shove-It bent toward my brother themselves. Aphra went through the line twice, waving in from her own car a few that hadn't shown up for the funeral, let alone signed in. Being helpless to control the signers must have compelled her to consider herding in these extra cars, ones I saw that contained just kids, nobody who would come on their own.

They all plodded along with us across the cemetery's unsold stretch to where the director waited under an awning. It was raining, an event that happened so seldom in this part of the country that the awning was dusty, causing a gray wash to slip off its front edge. Then, after what the director said and the clergy said and I said, because I was the closest after the parents, who said nothing, the rest of them saying whatever you say over such a hole, like how great he was and how he will be missed, and after we had all thrown in our bits of wet dirt and my mother had turned her back on it all to get to her flask tucked out of the car pocket, Aphra had to throw in a peach pit. Dead silence—you could hear that pit hit. The director said zilch about it, but you know it will sprout with this rain and be trouble to the mower. Nonetheless, weeping Aphra turned from the pit and its pit, and careened, like a storm in the Gulf, through all of us, coming adrift of my son, where she put her hand on his shoulder, where she turned him around to face her.

It was then that I saw how my son did have my brother's exact look after the medications wore off. Helping was a fresh haircut and the two inches my son had stretched since we moved here. Of course, the hand-me-down suit he stood in was handed down straight out of his uncle's closet, since nobody wore one around here except at funerals and nobody ever wore one out and what would you get for it at the Jumble Shop anyway but a quarter, and there wasn't a thing in town in my son's size unless it was ordered—that suit made a real difference in the resemblance, especially for those few who had ever seen my brother in a suit, or could imagine it.

She had taken up both of his hands in hers by the time I tapped her soft shoulder, my son in her grip and his head down and low, the way only an adolescent can tuck into a neck for effect. I told her that we were going home now for the wake and asked if she would follow us because we had so many hams and cinnamon buns given to us in our grief that the freezer wouldn't close. We wanted her with us, I said.

She pulled herself off him—hand over hand—and burst into more tears. She sobbed that it wasn't what we thought, and that she was so sorry.

It? I thought, and maybe others did too. We waited for more, but instead she swayed her big self through the rain over to where she was parked, walking over the too-smooth grass with its flat-to-the-ground markers just far enough apart to be side tables, places to rest your drink of water or a condom on, with a plush of grass between them so bed-like even I wanted to peel down the sod and crawl under.

My brother was dead was what I remembered then, and I cried a little the way a car does when the ignition's gone, a click and a grind, something that needs something, that could be stopped only by stopping.

Aphra didn't appear at the wake. She got lost driving over, or she followed some of those uninvited, unsigned-in elsewhere drivers for a wake of her own.

9

He had biceps like all the fruit they say the big ones are—grapefruit, watermelon—and lots of underarm hair that kept his smell close. He sweat a lot from doing pull-ups in the kitchen on a bar, one he installed just where you come in. I couldn't even get my hands around it, it was put up there so high. He would pull his knees to his chest, and slowly his arms would push his head past the bar. His face looked as if his brains were about to come through his ears.

He had a hard time with his brains, though he was smart. When he went off to college and had an exam, a spell would come over him and he'd forget everything he studied for. He had to quit. He didn't have to tell me about this kind of trouble—I saw. Sometimes when the covers were too hot, he'd seize up and his eyes, when I got the light on, would be rolled back like a horror movie. You are supposed to pull out his tongue if it gets in the way, but I was always too afraid of his teeth to try. He'd thrash around, making strange talk like I like milk *or* Too bad! Too bad! *That time with the* Too bad! *really shook me. It sounded like he knew he was doomed. The voice wasn't his. It was gleeful, as if his spell wanted to destroy him from inside.*

I decide on a small plate from the cupboard. The magazines say if you use a small plate, you don't take as much. I fill it with spaghetti I've just boiled, with a little sauce left that needs to be used. I swirl more pasta into it, and then some more sauce from the jar because there's not enough, and then a bit more pasta. And two big bites of celery in between to clean my teeth. I like how the pasta is both sticky and soft and how the cheese falls down like food dandruff.

Her brother always said smart people don't choose to be fat. Like, your mom is fat, too, so it must be in the family.

At the funeral, his sister ate the lipstick right off her lips. I wouldn't want to look like that, no matter how many funerals of boyfriends I had to go to. She wanted me to come over and eat pie with all the others afterward, but what did she want me to eat before with them? Nobody said, This is Thanksgiving—here's your place at the table, Amen. Not that I had moved in with him or had kids.

He said the problem with his brains was so bad that having kids wasn't the right thing to do. He did have a cat with a black tail that he spoiled with leftover toast and sometimes a whole bowl full of milk. That cat would look up at him with its ornery eyes for more and more milk. I saw the cat one day almost claw his face to get the whole carton. And what did he do? He held it in his arms for at least five minutes, close to his chest, wrestling it. It calmed down and licked his nose.

That cat didn't move in either. Some dog tried to.

I'm going to see if I can steal the Peace on Earth *sign he put in his front yard. Everyone thinks he left it there from Christmas, or to ward off those kids who put the pile of dirt on his lawn, but I think it's more for extraterrestrials.*

Sport, I say, come.

The car is thinking about it.

10

There's no other depression around like the meteor's for a hundred miles. Of course, you never see any of the actual meteor—what you see is a small crater with meteor rocks strewn around it, rocks that drive a compass wild. The meteor itself, all dust or pebbles from its crash so long ago, made that hole with its drop, one that holds the litter of time on top of it, bones and arrowheads and weed remains. Sometimes dust storms empty it out. Other holes farmers, even ranchers, bulldoze flat, making the top of the land smoother for their operations. But some holes are too low and depressed to bulldoze, like this one, and some are even more meteored. I read about it in this book from the library.

Did you have to wake me up to tell me this? my father groans from in front of the gray TV, where I too sit, paging through this new book I've checked out and read aloud from, thinking he had an interest, thinking he was awake.

It's just like his death, I go on anyway. A meteor blazes across the blue of an evening or a morning the world is not ready for, a meteor from some other bigger blaze. Or maybe not, maybe it is thrown by a baseball-capped god out of telescopic range—and that's that, impact. Nobody goes in looking for a black box to answer why it crashes unless it's a fat-cat scientist on a government grant somehow relating it to usefulness, the trajectory of hand grenades. Nobody's about to really investigate his death, right?

My father stands, stretches, and looks into my teacup at that drowned thing, the bag. You didn't think that much about him when he was alive.

I close the book and see a star lighting the back window. I'm going to sleep, I say. Good night. I can't say more, or I would say, What did you care then too? Sobbing at the funeral does not count. Why didn't you at least help him out of his miserable house, instead of collecting rent? But who shows how much goes into the care from a parent with a grown-up child, or even a lack of care? How much "hands off" is caring? I have a child. Maybe it even makes sense not to care. Sometimes.

I walk back to my room without turning on lights to make my father think, half-asleep, that what I said was a dream of his and not me talking: *Why did he die?*

It's not true that scientists don't want to know why things fall from the sky. Scientists are always wanting to know about what happens when things fall, especially if what comes down is from other places, alien places. I have told my son that aliens are just people you've never met or who come from another country, but a few people who live on this flat land here don't say that. They say meteors are vehicles for aliens and that aliens have landed with them and probably killed a lot of people in doing so, not to mention while wandering the world after their landing. If scientists don't want to know what happened with regard to a hole like this, these people do and will tell them.

What my father believes is that aliens for sure killed my brother.

Years ago, my father drove his pickup straight across some snow-blown flat road that the land has here, his spread at this point as much white land as you can squint into at one time, and my brother was riding with him, eating peanuts instead of breakfast, which is what you do if you haven't been on the inside of a grocery store for the last goddamn week because you've been working late digging postholes the way your father likes you to dig and because it is winter and no grocery store is open at that hour except peanut dispensers around the gas-up. The way my father tells it, when they get to the land beside the meteor hole and are driving along the fence line, eating peanuts and checking posts, a horse-trailer-shaped something comes hovering off the ground not a hundred feet away where there is no road, hovers higher, and zips off.

My brother, to the day he died, did not contradict him.

My father says, did say, Or else the government is up to something. It's one of those scientific tests they like to make, with dummies at the cockpit or helm, and barrels of taxpayers' money get burned to a crisp in the flash such a horse trailer makes exiting. He would say that and swear by it and forget it, except for what happened at the Snake House—what they call it instead of the Steak House because of the writhing can curlings you get in the soup if you aren't looking too close. The light when the waitress seats them looks great for pitch, but a little low for newspaper reading, although my father does try to read one right off, to see if there are any articles about government waste-of-money testing publicized in any of the back pages where they like to hide those things and say, *See, we published it.* Over the top of the paper, he notices two complete strangers take the booth behind them.

My father doesn't comment on the strangers at first, just sips the gritty coffee very quietly, just says *Pass* a couple of times, putting his paper down since it is honeymoon bridge they have taken to playing instead of pitch between newspapers. He listens, and my brother begins to listen too, because when do two total strangers ever come to the Snake House if they don't have to, if they can drive on by and eat anywhere else. These two are talking about government testing.

Swear to god.

They say, stiff as anything, *What did you think of it, Herb?* or someone else's made-up name. And the second guy says, kind of loud—but everyone is quiet, so it could have been in a reasonable tone, just regular talking—They're going to test five more like that this winter.

Then the two men go quiet, too, eating the special, which makes everyone quiet, looking for what might not be so special in it, and the waitress gets their desserts that the special requires, although she gets them mixed up, so they have to talk again in their strangers' voices. Then they stand up to pay, reaching for their wallets in their behind pockets.

That's when everyone turns to get a good look at them.

My father anyway, and my brother.

They were just two strangers, says my father and my brother, who used to nod there too, in my father's retelling, as if why wouldn't they be, given what they saw that morning? Then the strangers walk out and are never seen again.

And why would they ever be seen again? asks my father. They came to the Snake House to allay fear, to stop rumors. My father is sure they are not government plants; he is sure they are aliens trying to cover up their invasion. As my brother's death has to be covered up. So many strangers came to the funeral, that's another sign, says my father, certain after seeing that alien takeoff that he and my brother were always in great danger, especially my brother, and that the aliens would come to check to see if he were really dead. My father wears a copper bracelet to protect himself—from arthritis according to the quack he met who sold it to him, but my father swears it also works to keep off the intense radiation that sometimes aliens beam.

My brother would never wear one.

Took it upon himself, says my father. I went back to the crater to see if there were tracks—nothing. He shakes his head as if this is confirmation.

There wasn't a mark on him.

All those aliens have long memories, says my father. Time isn't the same for them as for us. He could be caught in time. They have accordion time.

Whenever he gets to this part, he pretends to play an accordion, and it is some sweet sad Bohemian song that has a polka inside it that no one can resist, especially since time and death are all that's worth singing about, even if you can't sing. He hums and we hum, the accordions of our lungs living synchronous and no doubt on the wane.

This is how he sees it:

An alien like some big ugly guardian angel has been lurking around my brother for a while, long enough so nobody's bothered, nobody notices anymore, least of all my brother. My brother goes to sleep one fine day to the next; then my brother does something stupid—or doesn't, like he stops going to the irrigation ditch that we know he does for no reason that we know of, except to pee, where he could be offering gin or food to the aliens or even to a god who, it must be said, like all gods, carries the odor of the alien on him, being that no one ever sees them or knows them too well. Or else he eats his offering instead of leaving it or drinks one of the beers he puts in the sand to cool for them. Or he just pees there, and that is the wrong place.

Anyway, my brother does something stupid, and the aliens pull the plug on him.

Not a mark on him.

It was a dark day, says my father.

It was late winter, I remind my father. No moon had crossed the sun, nor was anything else blocking it. It was seasonally dark.

Time is all you need, all you have, says my father. That's what they wanted from him. At least his medical bills were paid, he likes to add.

After the electrocution, there were a lot of bills.

11

His dad was someone who came around when I was in junior high. I never told her brother. Why annoy him when so much else happened to him, his spells, his car, his electrocution? It was nothing anyway. He was with a bunch of guys, and they were teasing me. It's a small town—who doesn't tease me? His dad was likable enough but just as married as everybody else. He thought I was swell but not for long. I was underage then and maybe trouble for people, making beds in that motel over and over. His wife wasn't the most friendly lady and probably gave him a hard time in the romance department, and certainly would give him the whatfor with regards to me, if she knew. After I was grown, I would see her at church not looking at anyone except ladies who had hats as nice as hers. My mom didn't have the money for hats—she wore a scarf like me. I guess if his mother had one hat better than anybody else, people would talk about it. But her son had zip, just like me. His house had a step down to the bathroom to remind you it was once a garage and could sure quick turn back into one. Anyway, the rent wasn't too bad. His electric wasn't bad either because he kept most of his sockets plugged, after the electrocution.

12

The space above the ground, way above, and the space over the grain bin, all over, was full of wires. My brother wasn't thinking about wires, he told me later, when he went to plunge a pole into the bin where stuck grain sat in the jammed-up auger. He thought pro-bin, get that grain to settle into it. He didn't think about falling either. The sway of the ladder so many feet up put more shove into him, not grab. He swung the pole up and out into all that space above to get more shove—and he got caught. That is, the wires caught the pole, and with that kind of catch—grabby—it discharges, and you fall.

Now, the thing about electricity is its exit. You may think that a jolt of that power—those are real wires, not just lines, and they clear him of the bin entirely, fling him through that great deal of air from high up to down, leaving a hefty stigmata on both palms where the pole touches—would be enough. But no. Electricity wants earth. So when his hand that held the rod held the current, in that thrilling moment when the sky offered its lit butt, the volts didn't squirm or relax or break off but thrust right through him, then out his hind end to where its straight line wanted to stop, to bury itself.

To bury.

It was no seizure. He had had seizures galore, and this was not one of them, a pop-branching inside his head and down. He said he had that thought and then a few more in the first minutes of reclining on his fractured back, waiting for anyone to come.

Not that anyone was there. The bin was and still is miles from anywhere.

He was stubborn and alone as always.

He tried not to look at his hands, but there they were, and raw. He didn't want to look at the wires, but they jittered and swung overhead, all in the motion of fun. Except for his back, he would have grabbed the pole and beaten the wires silly and then beat at the bin, because the bin had lured him up. Beating was what you want to do back in this situation. Except for the burns on his hind end and his hands. Except for his back. Instead, after the snout of those volts finished nosing him, both sides, he crawled to the shed, pulled the phone by its cord off the ledge, and skipped 9-1-1, going for the zero. Fourteen times he tried zero. You think about a lot, he said, a lot about zero when you are fried and can't dial.

The same way he went for the phone when he died.

With the land spread out so flat and even, people tended to miss the turn off or first left or first right to the farm. The volunteers drove past two sections, then put on the siren and drove faster past the—to them, townsfolk—featureless fields, until they reversed, until they found the bin finally and drove right up. Splints and tape will fix his back, they said. But they couldn't splint the in and out of current—no unguent they had would do it, nor juice for the fever that spiked with it. They strapped him into a plane just big enough for a gurney, and a pilot took him, jolting—ground, ground, air—somewhere better.

You would think parents at a party not so far out of town wouldn't think twice. The party was a reunion besides, people they saw every five years and not in between. But our parents had their lives: he was almost forty. And it wasn't as if this was his first accident—no, it was a wolf he had cried too often. All those seizure problems—this time it was just electricity. Of course he was fine; he had specialists where he was taken. They stood shaking their heads over scotch and talking of specialists, about how electricity went away—it wasn't a car body wrapped around a tree that had to be towed like before, or blood in a bathtub, or a finger lost on a freeway that needed sewing.

Even the phone service was okay, or he couldn't have dialed out, said my father.

Intensive care? I asked as if it were something I was afraid to purchase. I had flown to the hospital, trailing my own emergencies—a husband who wasn't speaking, a son who crawled in the corridor after me. I spent the waiting time asking, Does electricity fry everything on the way—flank steak to flank steak? Or, Remember the embassy in Russia that got cooked in the Cold War? Yes, it was rays, but what else is electricity? Talk like that carried, covered up the wolf business that made me feel foolish replacing our parents. But not too.

Besides pity, I had twin fear, that he was me and I might languish like this myself, alone. We were too close in age. And I loved him. It was instinct: the way a mate is dispensable, he was not. And he was good, the way goodness is a collection of symptoms. I listed to myself when and why: a birthday present, an opened door. But not too many of these good things or I'd have to forget the bad, so I pretended he was just my brother and no bother, like our parents. Except that it was I who was there, in the hospital corridor, caring.

What the nurses were saying was *He's talking*, they who didn't know how odd it was that my brother should talk at all, this brother who used words in abeyance, *in extremis*. A line must have been opened, with all the incoming current streaming out through his mouth. Unless the nurses meant screaming. This was, after all, the Midwest, where the nurses say, Excuse me, I have an emergency, as if it were UPS with a package they had to sign for.

In intensive care you can't get better than "satisfactory." "Excellent" goes elsewhere. Now exactly how soon to satisfactory, I was asking.

The nurses turned to the doctors, who licked their lips, uncommitted.

I didn't ask about death. I asked instead, How will you help him, with drugs or some surgery?

The doctors brightened and touched their finger whorls together. We will move his skin tomorrow, from here to here, they said, until it's very satisfactory. He won't look so burned—if he lives.

The nurses said, Excuse me, emergency.

We'll wait and see, said the doctors a day later. Let's have him walk first. Let him learn that first. There was nothing for me to do for three days but watch him in his cast lean into the IV and spot his feet the way a ballerina does twirling, and not cry. He did his three days of spotting while I waited for our parents to arrive. It is all right, I said to myself, having had my own son with me, for a parent to be finished being a parent. But I looked down at the toys scattered on the floor for my own, and I looked away.

When our parents finally arrived, annoyed by how long this was taking, I kissed them back from being alumnae and said how close this accident was and asked if there was anything else I could do, and then I left. After all, our parents were his *immediate* immediate family, not me, who had my own, now taught how to walk in the hospital foyer. My brother said as I left, There is nothing like electricity to bring people together.

Our parents didn't stay. Rather than take him home, they let him move to a nearby motel to save hospital expenses in recovery, and their trouble. In this space recommended as a last resort by the doctors, once a day a nurse took his temperature when no one else wanted it, and checked on his skin and the cast, or almost once a day. It was in this space where he lay with *Star Trek* and the news and did not dial zero again and again, but waited.

This was when Aphra became so important.

13

Easy does it, I told her brother every time he ran his hands along my outsides. You're a little rough.

I am hunting in the grocery now, where I want to buy a soft Easy Clean for Sport's outsides. Housewares?—I stop at the light bulbs.

He never picked up a fork without making sure he had rubber soles on his feet. He said not to wear any hat that poked up. That was pure invitation. Whenever it rained, forget about going out. Well, not everyday rain, but on days when the sky turned green, he really hunkered down. He shut the door tight and even turned off the lights in the whole house, as if light attracted lightning. Somewhere he read that electricity can come in through the sockets. If you're just standing beside them, that's not good either. Those sockets were taped off good, and all around. He bought a gas oven and threw away his electric. My present of a microwave never even got opened.

I said to him, This lightning fear isn't forever. You are going to get over it. After he was sick, I talked him into buying himself a really big luxury. It had to be plugged in, an item that tempted the electricity gods up the wazoo because there was water involved. Let's keep what it is a big secret, I said. Let everyone guess.

I'm going to the auction of it and his things, day after tomorrow, to buy myself a souvenir. The notice is right there, next to grocery checkout.

14

The auctioneer uses his face. Some of them try not to. Some of them just move the skin around their lips while speaking, the way a clarinet player puts danger into a tune, but not this one. He uses his face and works it.

Music does play in between each bid, however, clarinets and whatnot from the radio, as if to make much of each little lot of mismatched silverware, each hardly worn Sunday suit from adolescence on up, and its right tie. The things of a life are all clues to it. You put your arm up to your wrist into a bag of old shirts, and my brother is inside, as much as a person is inside anything. But my brother's books—a lot of them—surprise everyone, their backs so unbroken that his buying them at all is what's shocking. Most were collected from unread clumps lying around on the clean floor he always kept, with the bookshelves used for the storage of everyday changes of outfit, for shirts, ripped and smelly.

Some shiny shovels go for what they are worth.

So many people come because he had four beans more or some less than others and they like to see how he spent them, or else they come to see what mourning looks like on this set of people. They all look like friends, friends from the feedlot, the kids from the Stop-and-Go, the lawn mower man, even the priest. Some are good enough friends of the family that they think to ask, When's your mother coming back, and I say, Next week, as if I mean it. They and their wives bring nuts-and-bolts food, cake with impediments of raisins or actual pecans, hams socked with cloves. Everyone eats from their gifts and the others' while they stand inside, paddles up or down to the auctioneer, or they turn over the stuff in bins on the sidewalk and get it priced. All of them walk around the fill the Shove-It boys left, who are not—what a relief—in evidence. Two of the Shove-It boys have fathers who are wealthy, and I hear from a neighbor, one of the fathers is a cop, which is enough say in the town to have the making of the mound of fill in front of his place just an accident. There is one of the fathers now, kicking a cardboard box over to the fill. The younger boys like sliding down the mound on cardboard, all the way to the soft spring weeds that have sprung up and we have beaten a path through. They slide down as if it were snow and not dirt.

The neighbors carry their curiosity close, like something that can't be exchanged but that they can't make up their minds to keep. Already they want to use the toilet or at least drink from his tap. My father doesn't mind. He's not sad about my brother right now, especially with all this turmoil in and out of the house. His job is to direct those who don't want to bid back out to the sidewalk. Over there, he gestures to Aphra, who has turned up late but obeys and starts sorting through the things on display in the bins. I have found not a single thing that might be Aphra's inside, not a dropped pen with her initials on it, nor something with sequins for the bed. Did she clear out everything that might look like evidence before calling for an ambulance? Was he that tidy? Were they that unattached?

Out of one of the bins Aphra pulls a shirt of my brother's and goes behind a tree that the Shove-It boys have gashed, and tries to make the shirt fit over her. Of course the shirt gapes and loses buttons and seams until it is only right for the junk bin, until it is only right on her.

I watch through the window not far from the paddlers and the auctioneer's amp while someone takes her two dollars.

We have a Native American story in our family, one where we, or rather, the we that we were a hundred years ago, are looking out this window. Gallopers come up, not dressed well or overdressed in, say, feathers and makeup, nor are they making a lot of noise as if they are unhappy. They smile.

The Native Americans want bread.

They don't ask for the bread, but we, in the past, have given it to them. We are not generous every day or even now, and we give it not because they might kill us—that problem has been dealt with, overdealt—but because we know we shouldn't have ever built towns at all where they ride, we should just be visiting. *See you later* is what we should be saying to them, as if we were just passing through. But by then we've stayed long enough in their area to raise all of what goes into this kind of bread, and we want to raise more. Not to mention having a good start on all the graves.

They want the bread. At least.

We see in close-up, giving them our loaves, that although they are not so painted, they have painted their faces not so long ago. There is paint where it would surprise you, on their horses too, to make them spotted. While their horses lift their feet and they put up their hands in a salute, we also see that one of them is not what he appears to be—a woman—but is someone with whiskers. After they gallop off, breadcrumbs flying, we figure out that the one with whiskers is also not Native American and has robbed a train—Jesse James. The delay he and his gang made with the bread caused the cavalry to miss them, to trot right on by.

Time was all these scoundrels wanted with our bread.

My brother didn't have more time, disguised or not.

No one walking inside or down the aisle the bins make asks, *Did you find out why he died?* They pretend to come for what's to be sold, because such a question's answer might force bids higher. The auctioneer quips with that possibility at the tip of his quick tongue—Coming up is the hot tub!—for sometimes people will pay more for the true taint of the body. Anyway, they don't so much as bid for everything as wait for that last item. Some of them want it, but not everyone lives in a way that they could use it. This item is on blocks out by the garage, where a new car would have been if he had had the money to buy one, and no seizures. The crowd inside goes outside and floods over to the item. People like to inspect what my son had guessed correctly after the firemen came to put out its steaming, because of the round emptiness they see when they lift the lid, that possible death. I tell my boy not to ever sit inside one because maybe he is predisposed.

My son opens the tub anyway. He's a big boy—he wants to see if the inside bears a warning, a label that on a mattress you are not allowed to tear off. But of course, he is looking where everyone else has looked, to see if something of the body is somehow still in there. Four holes show where that label has been screwed off the way they do when it is a secondhand item, and no other label is anywhere else, either inside or out, not even the one warning pregnant women and small sweaty children about death deluxe in the amniotic waters of a hot tub. Nothing about seizures.

My brother had just left this tub at the time of his death.

But if he died from that hot tub getting him so hot that his brain fried, the papers that we have of his death would have said so. They just say his heart stopped, and it looks as if they mean it, although no one in this family has problems with their heart, at least not yet, and not him either that we know of.

People love the hot tub regardless. It is a grown-up aboveground item that shows you are aboveground with your wants and your wishes—just look at it. The auctioneer starts spieling. Someone who already has a hot tub but wants two bids higher and higher against a large family who could use an extra so the littlest can pee in the other one. If he who just does shovel work can have a hot tub, then they of course need more than one. Another one wants it just to have it and would put plants in it and say this is what happened in it.

We let them all bid. The money will go to a place in the country that keeps the country wild and undug, with his name on it. Or else my father will take it. He hasn't decided.

Soon someone loads it onto a pickup.

Not a mark on him and just out of the tub. No one believes that, but some believe that enough to want it and bid high.

My boy says he'll have to try one, and I say, Some girl will make you.

15

During high school I had a job folding and putting labels on new newspapers and then sticking them inside plastic. This is the kind of thing a small operation does by hand. I wasn't a newsboy, yelling out headlines as if I made them up myself. Boys did come in with their bags and their dirty old bikes to take the newspapers away and throw them at porches. You have to get up real early for that. But not as early as me. Her brother delivered for a whole year when he was twelve, but he hardly saw me, because I was older. His father, standing in the office, said a job like this one would make him a man. At least he drove him around on the snowy days when the plow hadn't gotten around to all the streets, and his bike was stuck. Before the boys came through the door, the papers had to be ready. Sometimes I missed school I was so tired with the deadline. I had a teacher, Mrs. Wellman, who said it was a shame I couldn't get to bed sooner, but she never let me explain. No other teacher noticed.

I could be smart, but without much sleep, the schoolwork was too hard. I could get the math done while the ink dried on the paper, but word problems and five-paragraph work? The press running full out was too loud to think, and Mom going on at home was the same.

It was take-on-a-student day a few years later that I finally quit school. I didn't need a take-on-a-student day. I was already took. His sister picked the newspaper to have her take-on with. She came in with a story she wanted to publish about catfish that walked on land that she had probably seen on a fancy family vacation to Florida. They printed the story, just like that. I had showed the editor a poem of mine over and over for about a month, about how sad daffodils are in the spring after they die, not that it was printed. His sister got her hands all dirty trying to look at the run too soon. The editor made a big fuss about the soap flakes she could use to wash with in the lavatory. I had to roll up the first good paper with her piece in it, stick it in the plastic, and hand it to her like a diploma. Thank you, she said, surprising me. She said it like I was a person who never needed school, who knew the ropes in a world that she didn't. That surprise and the fact that I got taken myself that night by the editor was what made me quit. The first meant I was all grown up, and the second meant I was popular. I think.

two

16

The dog holds his lit tail so high it's as if his tail wants to be let off—the dog can't hold it high enough while it burns.

I'm out of gas and stopped on a curve and thus can't catch or even follow that dog with its flaming tail dodging the light, dark, light of the blank, bleak shortcut highway near the meteor hole, nor the beige-black car coming up so close behind it that I think whoever drives the car must have lit that tail. I'm about to jump out to get them to stop chasing that dog, when that dog runs right past me, streaks away and back-loops the road. The flame doesn't die down, that flame someone must have made by sticking the tail into a tank and then, with some lighter, lighting it—that flame stays lit. The beige-black car with who inside hollering?—I'm distracted by the dog—slows and honks where I'm stopped, while the dog starts to circle itself, trying to bite that tail, then it runs back onto the road in front of me. The dog is too much on fire to run anywhere else other than to back-loop the road, which makes the beige-black car honk more, anxious to herd that dog along, with his lit tail and his gums bare, grinning like they do when we think they're happy.

Am I happy inside my car? When the dog hightails it close to me again, I crack the door to let it in, burning tail and all, crazy as that is, but the dog doesn't see me—the dog can't. The dog's seeing is hearing, because he's howling now, which is all anyone's hearing, window cracked or not, like those others. When he howls, his neck bends up toward his tail, making a U of terrible pain, and surely if I could see the dog's eyes the way his head is bent, I'd see them pop. What would I do anyway if the dog jumped into the car, tail lit, eyes popping, howling? I have no blanket or bucket of water.

I have only this much bravery—about as thick as the windshield glass between us.

I bend down and clutch the car mat.

The beige-black car creeps forward. A breeze teases the smoke from the tail into a swirl in front of it.

I step out and into the path of that car, with my mat and all my whatever bravery. The car swerves slowly off the road, then goes after the dog again, right onto the shoulder and farther. It drives the dog over a mound of scrub that's high enough to make the car's realigning a thump and puts a pause in the huzzahs made by the kids inside, whom I now glimpse. They are not yet fifteen like my son, or just, with just a license for learning, or maybe less. These are the Shove-It boys, and the pause that they make with their hung-up chassis is long enough that the dog makes a run past the shoulder, and that crazy, smoky torch he runs with touches the tumbleweeds ditched on the side, weeds waiting for flame—it's that dry. So a ball of, no, balls of fire light up as more and more weeds touch each other, touch that dog with his fire.

I chase the dog with my mat.

The torched weeds block the dog from me as their flames reach out of the ditch by the dozens. The dog, no longer honked at and now stopped by the car, reaches way around with that long neck dogs have after their muzzle and snaps at the fire that, thank goodness, hasn't spread up its back.

Its howls are screams. The boys in the car are laughing.

When these boys pull off the mound of tumbleweeds to get to the dog again, lit weeds attach to the car's underside, burning ones, and some of the weeds smack up against their grill where they grill, where quick flames, the only kind you get with these skinny weeds, lick. Flames lick so close to where the gas lies in its tank that they must have used it to light the dog, so close that the flames could light their tank, or that's what they might think. But they're not thinking, the driver especially, the one with a bare, hairless chest and I'm sure a beer can cold against his groin, who keeps turning the car around, his neck stuck out the window, noting the fire but thinking the car is his body, their body, all four bodies, and tries to shake the weeds off with his turning quick, thinking, if he thinks, that his turning will knock the fire off too, if his turning is fast enough.

They still laugh, holding the sills with their palms as the car doughnuts.

But this fast turning gives the weeds' smoky burn just a little more air, gives it just enough air to let it burst one more time into red and blue licks, and gives the gas inside just a little more heat past what a car needs for explosion.

The gas makes its whump of catching.

A sudden orange light fills the car, a cigarette-tip color. A boy's face turns to me, midlaugh. Another face replaces that one in the scramble out, the doors bursting open as they leave the car on fire behind them.

Boys on fire run past me, screaming.

I beat those boys with my mat, one and then the other. I beat them with my mat and my curses. I beat out the fire where I can.

The dog is gone so fast he's brilliant against the mindless prick of what-could-happen.

17

I wasn't there, I tell the officer when he comes around to ask, except for at the very, very end. I was on my way home from my place of work, the motel—you know the one clear off the highway?—when I saw the smoke and the boys. Yes, Officer, I saw a lot of smoke. It was all over their heads and mine, and drifting into the field. She was the one who stopped me. She sounded like a crazy woman, talking about a dog with a burnt tail. I figured it was a fire started by a farmer, the way they do it for safety, to get rid of field pests. But then I saw the car on fire.

The road is way out of the way, says the officer.

The officer is not from our town. They now have to hire someone not from here, because otherwise they found out no work gets done in enforcement, no arrests, no nothing on account of a local cop knowing all the locals, which means he doesn't know me at all personally, which is good.

I just happened to be driving around, Officer. It's a free highway, isn't it? None of the boys said anything about why they were burnt—they were so surprised. It got very quiet once I got them in my car. Some moans. I remember one of them said, Stop, stop, I left my phone inside the car, but I did not stop until I got to Emergency. It wasn't none of my business why that woman was there with those boys. They're all around her son's age, aren't they? Maybe her son knows something.

I bat my eyelashes, I do.

He looks as if he is tempted to ask me another question but struggles mightily.

I am a grown woman, I say. I have nothing to do with children. What dog did she say it was?

He takes off his hat and settles it back onto his head. Thank you, Ma'am.

Mom gets really angry after he leaves. She says she knew once she smelled the inside of that car of mine that I was in trouble.

18

How in the world did I come upon the dog? I was driving the shortcut, I tell my attorney, because I was short of gas.

I don't tell him how I'd been avoiding the shortcut, taking the long way, ever since seeing my brother in that dust storm a month ago. The heat rising from the asphalt of the shortcut as I drove and the surrounding twisted sage and other summer-loving foliage withering in the dust made a motion, a little life I feared seeing again. Thus distracted, I don't mention how that heat and the wavery light led my glance to a shovel. It was leaned up against my father's fence that kept the cattle from eating the sage and not stumbling into the meteor hole. I wouldn't say it glinted, but it sure caught my attention.

I was almost out of gas, and that was why I took the shortcut, that's all I tell him.

After I saw that shovel, I pulled off the road and walked out into the pasture. I made my way, staring down at my feet as I went, not wanting to look up and see the shovel held, my brother grinning under his cap. I could tell by the change from chunky road gravel to sandy soil and brush underfoot that I was almost to the meteor hole. Then I was standing over the shovel, having kicked it to make it fall from the fence, so it was more shovel, less him.

I'm supposed to dig into his past?

I threw the shovel over my shoulder and carried it to the car. It had to be his. I put it in the trunk, my dirt-dry hands wiped off on my pant legs, and I tried to get the car going again.

I just ran out of gas, I tell the attorney, and rolled to a stop.

But really I heard the car's innards slopping when I tipped onto the shoulder's gravel, so I was not surprised when the car harrumphed against my foot on its pedal and the dials confirmed *No gas*, not to mention my seeing a flash from a warning light miles earlier, although these lights often turn on at will, and not mine on this model. Here people often carry extra gas in their trunks since the distance between stations can be great. Gas is what people remember to put in after the lunch pail, after the extra coat or shoes. To me, having gotten used to plenty of stations, a can of gas can stink up a car, so I don't even think of taking one. I do mention this to the attorney, an explanation that puts him and everyone in town in a superior position vis-à-vis gas.

Or else my brother arranged for me to run out right there and find the shovel.

In the time it takes for me to look at those dials, in the time you wonder and fluster and turn the ignition again to On and the car still doesn't do a damn thing, in that suspended time between problems, that is when the dog and its tail sped toward me, followed by the beige-black car from around the corner of nowhere, out of my surprise and horror.

The boys say they didn't see a dog at all. If you're going to stick with the story about the dog, says my attorney, you're going to have to find the dog. Even Aphra didn't see a dog.

Aphra drove up after the dog was gone. That was after I beat the fire off the boys.

The attorney makes a note.

Aphra is the last person to save anyone, I don't tell him. That she should drive up just then in her too-big Buick, with a shirt of my dead brother's stretched over her bucket seat back like some skinny prisoner gutted and stretched to fit, made me fearful even then. Aphra doesn't go anywhere she doesn't have to.

The boys were screaming, I recalled for the attorney, having been rolled on the ground by me, the fire having finished with them by then, the fire having crisped its work and gone on. I dropped the mat and rushed over to my car. My phone was in my purse. I was about to 9-1-1 when Aphra drove up. I was so happy to see her I forgot about dialing and ran out to her. She had stopped a distance from the boys, who were now up on their legs and staggering. While I waited for her to roll down her window, me coughing from all the smoke, while I gestured and pointed at the obvious disaster, the least-burned boy got himself into my car. He was the one with the funny eyes—one dilated, one not—the druggy one, although there was the driver, with his burned bare chest that didn't seem to feel the burn at all, who just stood beside my car looking at his chest as if it were just interesting. Anyway, I had to get the kid in my car out is what I yelled at Aphra when she got her window down, I had to get all of them into hers.

But why? she asked me.

Gas, I said.

Then the burned screaming boy with the problem eyes wouldn't get out of my car, although I asked him twice. Two of the others couldn't walk very well, but they were headed for my car too. No gas, I yelled at them, waving my arms, and then Aphra yelled too. I was so crazy in the smoke and the screaming that I just dragged that screaming burned boy out of my car and put him into Aphra's, into the back seat with all her trash, and crowded the rest of the boys in around him.

They were losing pieces of flesh if you touched them, they were shedding already blistered bits on the car handle. I don't tell that to the attorney.

All Aphra did was ask, Is your son in here too?

I said no. I was in shock. You'd think I was burned too.

Then she drove off with the boys.

Thank god she stopped is what I thought then. I found myself walking upwind with my mat in my hand toward my car, the fire rising behind me, when the fire trucks showed.

She must have 9-1-1ed. I forgot.

I look around at the attorney's office, so certificate-framed and anxiety-decreasing in wall color, with a secretary at his entrance to keep out creditors, the blonde woman now seated next to the chair-filling man, both of them staring at me.

The story is the story of the town for the next two weeks. Aside from the Shove-It boy with the father in the enforcement end of the law, just as I'd heard, two of the burned boys come from families with big money—their cattle can take your cattle—and their kind of family is not happy to have their boys accused of such a thing as dog-burning. It puts them in line for a Class IV felony, not to mention cancels their claim of a car accident with the insurance people. Better the problem be me and the boys having to maneuver around my car parked in the middle of the road—which is not where it was at all—and thus their catalytic converter catching fire in the stubble they had to drive through. Besides, the boys were burned on my father's land, which the two wealthy parents want for its hunting and fishing and which they had bid on earlier to buy and lost. My father had posted it with no-hunting signs and one day confronted their guns with his own. Looking for pheasants? was how he put it, but these hotheads, the attorney relays, construed his being armed as more than a fellow hunter inquiry.

On top of that, the attorney says that when they file, they'll come after me for personal injury for beating them with the mats. Mayhem, intent to maim. Far-fetched, but that kind of fetching has its backers in a small town, although you would think that the death, if not the electrocution, of my brother would create a sympathy that would overarch.

Why was it Aphra who found me?

She found my brother too. All she says about that, and she says it whenever she can, is that she was the one who kissed my brother last. Okay, whatever. But what was she doing there on that day that she found him to kiss him? And what did that have to do with her finding me at the scene of the burned dog?

You have to find the dog, repeats the attorney.

The boys' parents are trying to have me thrown in jail. I suspect what they have thrown already is money at the prosecuting attorney, who is only paid by the state after all and has eight children to feed and, I understand, is a dog owner. No one cares why Aphra was there—she has no sunflowers or crop that could be theirs, in settlement.

My story about the dog is not altogether the one that people expect.

My son is occupied by his screen when I return home from the attorney's. My father is napping. He naps well and long, and that makes all the difference in the tenor of the rest of his day, which leaves only my son to help me search for the dog. Driving anywhere with me is the last thing my son wants to do—unless he's the one who's doing the driving, given that his permit is only a learner's. I should not be searching for the dog at all. I should be bent over my own screen, tracking elevator money, but it is something of a holiday, to be suspected. He protests, saying he can only do left turns, and I say we'll circle.

He drives along in sullen silence. I tell him the investigation's getting serious, the way cops do on TV. But really, I add, I have only two weeks to produce the evidence so the judge at the preliminary hearing can dismiss all of this. I haven't been back to where it happened—why would I?—although everyone and his cousin has been there to sightsee, or at least drive by the charred brush. You would have thought by now the dead dog might have been found. But how fast I remember it zipped past the smoke and the fire—right through some of it.

As soon as we find the dog, you can go back to your game, I say.

Whatever, he says, and pushes sixty-three in a zone meant for fifty-five, and he smiles just a little.

How fast could a dog run in such a situation? The only reason it stayed on the road was because of the car's honking, and that's another thing these rich boys' parents' lawyers are saying I made up, these boys' honks and their swerves, not only the lighting of the bushes by the dog. But what else causes a fire to start under a car, other than a dog on fire whose tail caught on the weeds? There was a dog and there was fire and they honked and scared it—and probably lit it.

If you see anything, let me know, okay? I say.

Of course he has my brother's profile when he's pretending to be put upon. Anything? The door handle? I see sticks with red flags—does that count?

If you listen to his speech, his duh, duh, da-da-da, you hear he hesitates like my brother did—he is a vessel of his voice trying not to show his excitement. The world stops to listen during such hesitation, and I, for one, hear my brother and his voice changing but then, in the next live breath, my son and his young voice. He must have listened to my brother hard to sound so much like him—or else it is just the voice of his same-sized body. While he asserts with fervor that few of his friends have to spend this kind of time with their parents, I scan the land.

You can still scan all the land at a glance and move on—it's that flat. I was lucky to notice the shovel sticking up, since it was camouflaged against the fence post. A dead thing like a dog would lie unnoticed here, and though birds might mark the spot for a short while, there might be only mice droppings to show what fur was left, another dog already gone and happy with the bones, or ants en masse at it, or just flat-to-the-ground worms to alert me.

But there is the brush to mark where the car blew up—blackened and twisted, with the glass of a popped windshield all around it, what's left over after the rest of it was towed to a car grave. I don't want to stop. No. But my son cuts off the road, the weeds *shshshsh* the car's underside.

Okay, here.

He stops, and we stare at all the weeds left to crush, at the road left behind in my rearview, at the remains: plastic this and that unwanted by the recycler. I get out and shade my eyes and stride around. Along with back-seat webbing, I see a candy wrapper, probably exploded out of the car or flung out of a window by a sightseer. Or blown from Aphra's car. My son yells from our car that the fire department put the fire out pretty fast, but he can't resist getting out himself and kicking at the char. I agree with him about the devastation: not much. There's some scorching of the ground where it first caught, but already the wind sifts the black in with the brown, a brusque wind that whips and moans.

Bugs sing just below it. They can be heard fine when the wind stops.

Already the burned and bandaged Shove-It boys drive around town in someone's dad's old Cad. They shake their fists at me whenever they see me or, worse, pull up too close. They keep saying I am the reason for their being burned. But I notice this Cad now comes with a grill protector in front, one that could ward off any bushes that could alight, an admission of fire hazard from someone other than myself. For that kind of boy, my son has his own grill protector, a skateboard. Those boys don't skate. My son's friends skate and then loll about the house with their boards. You're all out of line, out of alignment, I tell them. They like to address me as Mrs. and ask first whether it is all right to eat the six burritos in the freezer, and of course I say yes like I meant them to have them when I bought them.

You know, my son says when we get back in the car, our class did a dog in the last week of biology. My teacher said he was going to throw out the whole skeleton.

I don't know, I say, if another dog would work.

He sighs and puts the car back into motion, drives the circumference of the burned place in country roads, one grid inside another, drives off into a ditch where there seems to be a hole leading somewhere and scares a snake, turns left at the grain bin that my fried brother waited so long beside, says he is happy to drive back to the site and start over. A pheasant, a brown-, red-, and black-tailed male, flies up out of the brush in glorious color, and we miss it. Then he drives to where a hawk circles what?—a tossed-out bologna sandwich.

What kind of dog was it? he asks.

Could've been brown. Medium-sized.

The bones of the school dog are probably right there in the trash, he says. I'm just saying.

I am just a woman, I sigh. Why do they think anything of me?

Ah, the "just a woman" defense, says my son, staring out the window despite himself, searching. You should turn it around—the dog should defend you, the way they're supposed to.

I guess I could just about put bones anywhere. And if I burned them a little—

Bones are on the inside, he says with disgust at my dimness. The color of the bones doesn't matter. You'd be better off chewing on them. But wait a minute—they might get somebody with a PhD to DNA them, to check for cinders.

You watch too much TV, I say with all the assurance of someone who seldom watches. The county wouldn't pay for that.

Maybe, says my son. But it's not as if they're going to find the dog themselves.

19

He liked to follow the stock market. He said it was about gas and plastic and national debt. He said it showed the worries of everybody in the country. Like a pulse, he said. He would take my wrist and so gently hold onto it between his fingers and say the Dow was definitely up. He taught me how they short stocks and how they average down, about bears and bulls, blue chips and margins. Strange stuff for a country boy like yourself, I said to him.

Not that he put any money into the market. I like to watch, he said. Why, I made $4,800 last week on two shorts I thought about. And we would drink to that, freshening up our beers with a new one. That was the closest he ever came to gambling.

Once I was the one who followed his tips, and the market took my whole week's pay before I could even spell C-H-E-A-T. He said, You're just unlucky—it's about luck. When I went to put the money in, I found out the broker in town was a kid-glove man. His secretary wouldn't let me through the door. They have a kind of narrow door anyway, on account of the fact that the office is pretending to be fancy, with columns, but the doorway wasn't built right. Columns, here in a town where most people are happy to have roofs! I had to send them a letter with a check inside to get them to do anything. That slowed me down and it's all about timing. When I did it again all by myself online, I made over one hundred dollars. Better than a poke in the eye.

20

My son knows just where in the summer rubbish the bones were left, and since the janitor considered end-of-school rubbish not his, they remain where they were tossed. My son uses our toast tongs behind the janitor's back to remove them. They could have been last year's edition of an up-to-the-minute biology book that he brings home on his bike in a box, except the weight inside clatters when he hands it over.

I choose the most beat-up big bones out of the lot of them, I tease the neighbor dog into gnawing on a few for effect.

The next night when I tell my father I'm going to "pick up supplies," he doesn't say the grocery store's been closed for an hour. He's settling into a comfortable chair and asks for batteries to make it shake or tingle, whatever I can find to change it to work like one of the better recliners. Sure, I say. My son says to me in the kitchen he's done his part, bringing in the bones. He says his job is now to work out ideas for a summer project on the phone with someone he talked to during the last week of school. He even turns down driving me to the site, so I know he's serious about whomever on the phone—or seriously afraid of getting caught.

Nobody has batteries this time of night.

So it is just me planting the bones, arranging a few of the best into a sort of inviting circle, with bacon grease smeared on the tips to attract whatever might weather them further. I kick up the dust around it, and drag a tumbleweed over.

I have to do this by night. If I do it by day, low-flying trick planes from a fair or crop dusters will swoop over and land and ask directions, trucks will park and their drivers will decide to go for a hike instead of peeing on their tires, two cars coming from opposite directions will not avoid each other and crash, attracting emergency firefighters, rubberneckers, volunteers from all over. If I do it by day, my father will catch me, and I'll have to say aliens made me do it.

Thank god it is dark enough. A filmy Milky Way doesn't add up to the light of a whole star, and only satellites hover in the baggy dark bottom of the sky. The bag of bones constellation, I call it.

I don't want tire tracks right next to the bones, so I've parked on the no-print asphalt and trudged a long way out into the pasture, relying on a sinking moon for light and where the fence posts come together to locate me. Now it's just these scattered clouds all the way back. I sure could use something with batteries myself right now—or a meteor or a really bright-lit tail.

Some canine yips.

No dog I can see. Then I'm near enough to where my brother stood last—why can't I stay away?—and I get spooked. While I wait for the clouds to rearrange so I can see, I block out the newer memories—the screams of those burning boys—with takes on my brother:

Small and furious at six, dog-digging in fury because my father swore he couldn't dig to China—a digging inspiration if there ever was one—he found a popped firecracker not two inches down, all the Chinese writing rolled up inside, proving everything.

At eight, the books he memorized every word of so we wouldn't know he couldn't read from all the little spells interrupting his brain, and how I tricked him, turning the page in the wrong place so everyone would know he couldn't.

What color were his eyes really? Red, from sneezing. He had allergies, and he dug into the soil anyway, mold and hay and hot winds full of alfalfa notwithstanding, sneezing so much the shovel would fall from his hands and he'd trip over it, pulling out a hankie.

I wouldn't call him clumsy. When he was twenty, he took a pot of burned chili Mom made over a bonfire and set it out on the ice, to skate a circle around it. Said he would skate until the ice separated into a floe and we all sailed away. An ice bump did upend him then, and in the tangle, he sliced his finger almost in half.

Unlucky. Mean-spirited. Vengeful. Once he gave me his piece of pie.

He was always turning off the lights. Whether you were in the middle of threading a needle or finding the last piece of a puzzle.

I grope through the dark until, at last, I find my car.

21

She drives around late, when only people sneaking around drive, or people up to regular no-good boredom. I'm in the second department, but that's not important.

I don't follow her.

Her car at the light interrupts my dreaming about her brother, whispering to himself about stocks. We would sit in my car to listen to the late reports that came on around this time and imagine the market with men throwing slips of paper into the air around their computers.

I can't help but wonder where in the world his sister is going. There's no takeout in this town. No late church committee meetings. The Lions Club and the Elks and whatever other animals don't meet this way, and they're men-only.

She's in trouble with the burned boys. It must have to do with that.

I drive out to where the accident happened. Nobody else on the road at all, so she must've been quick and gone home the other way. When I shine my lights over in that direction, I see only some poor creature creeping off into the weeds. It has such a bad limp I'm afraid to get out and look, for fear it will attack me out of plain pain. I don't know that it could be a dog, but maybe.

22

Here they are, I say to the prosecutor a few days later, after he follows me out to the crime scene. I say we're lucky there's anything left—that rain last week we had could have washed it all away.

He marks the area with tape like there's a dead person asprawl and takes a couple of pictures of the laid-out dog bones. He does wonder at how quickly the flesh disappeared and where the fur is. And a skull?

I shrug. There are animals.

These bones could be a big raccoon's, he says. He isn't the county prosecutor for nothing. He puts a bone into a bag and seals it with tape. I'll let you know what the lab says, he says, but I know that he is the lab and that working out such things is not the fun he probably thought he'd have after getting out of prosecutor school.

Next week? I ask.

Could be, he says. Could be. In the meantime, don't you go anywhere.

I tell my father I see the dog running in the distance all the time now. It's always too far away to tell for sure what it is, a blur at the edge of the tint of the windshield, a twinkle where the sunset runs out. Even if the fire died long ago—which of course it has—that dog still runs where I can't quite see it.

Seeing things is a sign of old age, he says. All you can do is close your eyes.

He closes his for a nap.

I can't close mine—I'm driving again. We're on our way home from the cemetery, where we left a few early asters for my brother in a bouquet beside the stone. On my back seat is a ticket stub from a trip to Vegas. I found it today at my brother's house, tucked into the shoebox in his closet, with his name, a date, and *all paid for* printed in the right places. I took it along, as if visiting the cemetery would explain it.

Why would he go to Vegas by himself? my father asks, rubbing his eyes.

Maybe he was lonely, I tell him. Lonely people go there.

The mob did it to him, says my father.

Not aliens. We don't talk about aliens much anymore unless sadness wells up in him like the weeping of a wound and he needs his alien Band-Aid.

I nod as if I agree about the mob. Maybe Vegas was the place for him and not only for his loneliness, I say. I mention whole afternoons when he cornered me in the basement, tossing down the little lead roulette ball or the dog-eared cards, taking in money with the hands of a magician, remembering the suits, years of double or nothing allowances. It wasn't gambling—he always won, at least with me.

All that pitch we played at the Snake House, says my father, staring at the crops that are going by. I let him win.

A gravedigger knows the odds, I say. I doubt it.

He closes his eyes again. I glance at the ticket and back at the road. I imagine Vegas ladies on a hotel TV chanting with their lips synched, their outfits slipping, then not, my brother, who stays with those ladies, his hands open, ready for the ladies' feathers, and once he catches a feather or it falls off into his hand, a plume of red marabou or a word like it that the mouth must cup around, if only air, and he's happy. He mouths *boudoir*, all pursings and cuppings, and sinks farther into the bed. He lets his shoulders tighten while he mispronounces it, and still the bed's poor springs resist like a girl, like his mouth with the French and the smile until he sleeps, all pursings and cuppings over, the endpoint of thrill, the feather's undoing.

Or he is lying on the felt, and he's betting on himself. The croupier lifts his rake, and the ball drifts—red, black, one, two digits, odd, even, even, black, thirty-two. He doesn't need to stretch his neck and look over his shoulder; the big rake lowers over him with the croupier's *Thank you very much*. All he has left he spends on a creamer made in China.

Or he is hung over in a Vegas beauty parlor, head down on a manicurist's stand, the red-hennaed ladies getting touched with red on all their tips—there's one with nipples red lacquered and hair a soft flame against a blower. They don't wonder why he asks for a drink the moment his head is lifted. All he wants really is to see his reflection and his smile in the lifted glass.

Telephone, Eileen. Telephone, Anna.

He has a telephone in his head, and all the women whisper to him. They say, No, no more drinks. We'll be open tomorrow. Yes, and maybe.

He doesn't like this *maybe*. He puts his head down again. He just listens.

Anna says he's a wino, *no dinero*.

Eileen doesn't agree. He had a wallet when he came in, I swear it.

Let's truss him up and find it. You do it, Eileen—you're the one. Or I will, you know, do something else.

He can't see which one will do that something else, without himself moving. He says, Why not? and it's free fall from then on, death big-time, all the legs lifted, panties off. And then the mob rushes in and throws him into the back of a car, no clothes on, not a mark on him, and then they drive and drive and drop him home.

Maybe he told Aphra that he really didn't like her, after he returned from his trip to Vegas, that this time, even more than after his return from that mysterious town, he really wanted to be left alone. She would have motive. But to kill him? Then he was electrocuted and she really had him.

So what do you think? asks my father, holding the canceled Vegas ticket close to his face, awake again. Mafia?

No, Dad, I say. No.

In Vegas the Mafia have a game of bluff that the blind aren't allowed in, my father says. The eyes talk, and that's how the house keeps its profit up, letting them. Whiskey makes the eyes easy to read, although most drinkers seem to think it confuses them into mistakes.

But he was a one-drink kind of guy, I say.

It's hard to get mixed up in the Mafia sober, he says.

When we are talking like this, at the windshield while I drive, he can talk into it, straight, but I can talk straight into it too. I say, He thought it was you who would do him in.

I want to know if my father knew this, if he aided and abetted my brother's fear of him, maybe a usual fear between fathers and sons, maybe always sublimated, but still real. My brother told me about it after he quit college. He feared my father's helpless anger at his spells, especially after his electrocution. Why couldn't my brother control his electricity? Why couldn't he be someone else's son?

Your brother didn't know himself, let alone me, says my father.

You never regretted not taking him home after the hospital?

Regrets, he says, are little deaths—nail, nail, nail. He pretends tapping on a coffin. You can't have them.

After a silence so long he's turned the car radio on and off, I say, I am always looking for clues.

Me too, says my father. He'll be standing in a field like in that picture Grandma kept on the stairs.

Millet.

His head will be cocked, so you know he can hear his bell from the church.

Or maybe the smoke alarm's ringing, his toaster oven left on again.

He left it on all the time, says my father, punching my windshield wash jets and then the wipers as if that's what gets rid of tears.

I found a syringe too, I say. I looked through the trash when I went to put up the *For Sale* sign.

It must have been a bad pollen day, my father says. He gave himself shots.

It was in the end of winter.

He was allergic to everything, says my father. He hated farming.

We pass my father's early sunflowers, a quilt of green and yellow all nodding one way for six miles. He usually reaches over and honks—to wake them up—but today he stares at the windshield that absorbs what he feels, not interested in talking about the syringe or the hospital anymore, dismissing them with more talk.

Reality is not about what you see, he says when we turn into town. The philosophers all agree on that. Even when they say *This is real* and why, it's always about what isn't real, that whatness they regret they can't see behind their backs that makes them regret saying anything. Philosophy is all about regret.

I'm sorry I said anything, I say.

Reality is like a magic trick, he goes on. It's always up your sleeve. Think about how Shakespeare showed reality—he would set fire to curtains.

You mean the characters would get stabbed for standing behind them, I say, finding our block. And then there was revenge.

People shouldn't have to die just because they were listening in. Even if it worked for Shakespeare. My father fixes his glasses, another sign of tears. We're all just moons, listening in. You should look more at the moon, he says.

I stop the car just a fraction from the garage wall. We take in the tin can that held the flowers we dropped off. I head for the kitchen to fix a cheese sandwich. My father says a cheese sandwich will release, if not morphine, then endomorphins of comfort.

Endorphins, I say.

You can eat those too, if you want, he says. He's now standing beside me, opening a package he's fetched from outside. Here, these are fresh out of the TV.

He holds up two smoked carp that curl toward him in parentheses. Since my brother's death, my father will smoke anything, even mushrooms once, having popped up in his smoker one spring, but not on purpose. He ate them anyway. This summer, a neighbor had a surfeit of fish, so many they didn't fit in his coffin-sized freezer, and he offered them up to be smoked too. I tell my father poor white trash smoke things, but he says chefs in big restaurants want all his secrets. Smoke curls out from inside anything he finds that will work as a smoker. A TV console was a good bet, and it worked fine.

He lays one of the curly fish on the counter. If you didn't dwell on your brother so much, he starts.

Someone has to. I sniff the fish. His is not such a closed case. You, on the other hand, are a nutcase. Look at these things. This isn't food—it's embalming.

When he smiles, my father's age pleats into his face. Otherwise, he could be forever seventy, white-stubbled and pink-skinned up to his own *Feed and Seed* cap.

Now, where would Mom put a sharp fish knife? I ask but not without hesitation. My father is sensitive to her being gone for so long. Usually just a month dries her out.

He lifts a shoulder in a *Who knows?*

I grip the edge of the fish and cut it with the knife we use for paring, a serrated one that chops bits off fine.

Why do you think Aphra turned up just in time at the fire? he says between fish bites.

Finally, someone asks me, I say. Because she is everywhere, a goddess in disguise?

Don't blaspheme, he says, pulling a smoked bone out of the side of his mouth.

A town is too big when you can't suspect everyone, I say. Or me, I say.

My son saunters in. I smell remains, he says. He sits in front of the second fish and wolfs it down, bones and all, a sign he is not so thoughtful, because ordinarily he would question the nonbeef aspect of such a piece of food, its smoky presentation. Maybe your brother got hit on the head and the bacteria got loose.

What?—asks my father—Were you listening to us? the way old people ask, never expecting eavesdropping, having given up on being heard.

There was no sign of a blow, I say.

My son shrugs. I think he slipped in the hot tub and hit his head just enough that it released some bacteria that got him just like that. The bacteria was in him already, and the heat from the tub made it go crazy with reproduction, you know—it just took over.

What do you think, Dad? I ask.

He purses his lips. Skip the cheese sandwich, he says, I'm full. He slips his fish skeletons back into the bags that they came in, finds the trash. I am taking your son out, he says in fresh declaration, for a real driving lesson.

My son's licensing is four weeks away. You just got home, I say.

He needs to learn the finer points, not wheat-field driving, not the legal stuff they taught you last summer, he says. Your mother is neglecting your education. You can make good money driving if you know all the tricks.

You know good money that needs driving around? asks my son. The queen maybe?

My father's lonely, driving around all day looking at fields by himself without his son, is what he could answer, but that would turn the grief he's accusing me of into his own. A parent must be strong, stronger than his children. He doesn't have grief or regret—you can see that from the way he changes the subject. He says to his grandson, I can help you learn backing up, if you want.

It's not as if he ever took my brother out to learn to drive.

But when my father takes off a pretend hat and opens a pretend car door, I can't resist and raise a pretend skirt and carefully board what he is going to pretend drive, a car twenty feet long.

Okay—let's get on with it, says my son. I have pavement to burn.

I stay turned away while they leave, because if I see my son's big back behind my father's, with the two of them together, it's my brother's back.

No bacteria were mentioned in my brother's report. Not a one.

23

When that Vietnamese woman puts out the food at the All You Can Eat and looks at me that certain way, I go all Wonder Woman, and thunderbolts flash from my fists. Who do you think you are? I am big, so much bigger than you—I can crush you. Then that big power backs up and zaps me instead of her, all because of shame. This can happen when anybody watches me pick out food and how much I take, even if it's hardly anything. The Vietnamese lady (Dep is her name—you've got to name your enemies), she always watches.

My mom used to close me up in the pantry when she was mad. It's real small with just shelves to hold things like unopened ketchup, but it used to hold me nice and close. Pass me the honey, Mom would say from the kitchen, but you can't come out yet. Mom was fat too. She punished me for eating the leftovers she wanted or even for not washing my hands enough. I fooled her, didn't I? I got so I could eat flour from the bin all by itself, and I drank the tops off the spaghetti sauce and screwed the lids back on. Even dry noodles can be good. Anyway, Mom would let me out after hardly an hour, because she missed having somebody to complain to. Sometimes she'd have to pull me out—I liked it so much inside there. I really liked being left alone.

Whenever Mom feels down, she eats a half gallon of ice cream in front of the TV. I have to help eat it so that it isn't all her fault. Eating alone, she says, is just like drinking alone, not so good. Then she shuts me up in the pantry because I am getting fat too. After a while I didn't fit inside. We only had one other closet, and it was completely full of coats and boots and the space heater and stuff to clean the house with. The kind of cleaning I really needed was a squirt bottle of something to make shame go away, and that turned out to be him. Beration nation! he said. I don't want to hear it, he said. A hundred years ago if you were skinny, it meant you drank too much or you didn't want to work for food or were sick. It was bad to be skinny. People stared. He said he saw people looking at him like that just before he went into a spell, and for sure when he got out of one.

I once caught someone looking at Dep that way, a you are different *look, which is why she comes to mind. I did think then, Serves her right, but I'm trying to do better.*

Once Mom and me went to buy something stretchy, because elastic is supposed to make big look good. I got stuck in a pair of stretchy overalls, went into the wrong holes, something, and she got stuck in a pair of pants that didn't fit. We both crashed into each other in the dressing room trying to undress, which tangled us worse, and even worse when we laughed so hard.

I take Sport for a little drive-around.

24

Sitting behind a steering mechanism that purports to control the car by means of grasping it firmly or, in the case of my son, casually—two fingers and an occasional heel of palm—and pressing down on the pedal, which engages the pistons that produce the roar under the buttocks of the said smiling son, and staring out the windshield, which both permits the sitter to see for steering and perhaps shields him momentarily from impalement upon, say, a mailbox, is a youth's right and must be exercised, especially prelicensing on any and all vehicles, so help me god.

There ought to be a law.

No longer does anyone pull up in a cloud of dust, even in our small town, unless there's a storm, and then the dust is sucked out of the fields, the town's mouseholes, any small acreages not yet slicked down with tar, and it suspends itself everywhere. A certain shriek of tires, a wheeze of brake is all that announces my son's return. This carefreeness is also an announcement that no money has been saved up by my son for his own car—unlike his uncle—not one penny from the creamer is thus earmarked.

You're home early, I say to my son, who plants himself at the table while my father squares the pickup in the garage. How'd it go?

Good. My son finds and hunches over his cereal bowl so deftly I can't see how full he fills it, the amount of milk that follows.

I speed up the dinner part of the meal—I stir and I chop.

We drove up the hospital hill and down, he says after three dips of his spoon. The pickup worked fine. It was fun, he says, so I know the vehicle was barely under control.

My father waves *No bother* at me, joining us.

I fuss with a potato. And?

Then we had to ditch Aphra, says my son. He pretend-twists a wheel with violence.

She came at him, all puckered up as if she was going to give him a kiss, says my father.

She got out of the car at the light, says my son.

We drove slow to get her to back away from the window, says my father. I didn't know what to make of her.

I nod in complete agreement.

My son finishes what will take the rest of us at least another ten minutes, if not another snack, and lurches out of his chair.

Jell-O? I offer, cutting off his exit. Dessert before dinner? I tantalize, to get more story out of him. I happen to have it made, I say, as I do now and then in honor of Uncle Beck almost inventing it and, of course, in honor of the Jell-O cushions.

The family jewels, my son says, extracting four globs from the fridge-released bowl. He suctions the Jell-O off his saucer standing up and spoonless.

Aghast as usual at his eating antics, his grandfather and I murmur what could be taken for admiration or pride but in truth is inhaled disgust. My son knows better, but this kind of knowing is so time-bound that it will take years to register. He thinks we can't hear him eat this way, just as he refuses to hear our objections.

My father forks his own Jell-O.

I turn up the heat on everything, on the off chance someone might want to actually eat what's on the stove, and I wait. The silence during and after eating this dessert always inspires revelation, perhaps due to the sudden unfulfilling quality of mere water and sugar and the horses hooves of Jell-O.

My son, sliding a second helping onto his plate, says that the last thing Aphra said while they were driving off was that she was going to SACK, and did he want to come?

As in "sad sack"? I ask. Or "to be sacked."

My father makes *I don't know* with his hands, his mouth full.

My son turns his own full face toward me just as the last of the Jell-O makes its way from his cheeks down his throat. She was after me, like I said, he says after his gulp. What's it mean—S-A-C-K? Is it something I should ask my friends about and not you?

SACK is some new group, I remember, knowing now he's right about who to ask. It stands for Sexually Abused Children and Kin. But you got an A in health—you know all about that subject.

My best, he says. Let me draw you an ovary.

We're still eating, says my father.

She wasn't abused, at least not at home, I say. What I heard was that her father died or else left them right after she was born. I could be wrong about that. She didn't have siblings, and her mother, as far as I know, lived like a nun, struggling to make enough money to feed her. Maybe those stories about high school boys were true.

Never second-guess, says my father, his eyebrows up in accusation. Although she did have some reputation.

He helps himself to seconds.

I spoon out the rest for myself in solidarity—and despair, my son nosing around the fridge for whatever else isn't dinner.

Not that he won't eat the dinner too.

I'll bet Aphra goes in for the free treats that all those groups serve at the end, my son says, looking into the now gelatin-free bowl in his hand as if I could instantly refill it. Things like Cool Whip with pretzels mixed in. He lets the fridge door shut.

Ah, Cool Whip, says my father. I thought it was actually made from pretzels. He excuses himself as if it were actually a meal that we have eaten, to find the mail.

I think what they really do at SACK is drugs, I say when my son and I are alone. Kids make drug pickups there, right? I watch my son for a telltale flinch at the no-no word *drug*.

He eyes me back. Hey, they're sexually abused—what do you expect, heavy petting?

I laugh, and it's fun, this son with his new grown-up wit. I need to know how grown-up. I say, Could SACK be where my brother got the syringe?

It was for his allergies, says my father, popping around the corner with a bundle of envelopes, bills, and circulars.

Syringe? says my son, all ears.

I open the silverware drawer, which neither of them ever open, and pull out a plastic bag ziplocked the way cops and TV detectives close it. I even hold it out the way they do, with two fingers, as if my prints are going to burn through the plastic.

What do you know? says my father.

Anything left in it? My son angles himself in its favor.

It's all dried up, if there was ever anything in there. I stopped at the police station to show it to them, but you know, the certificate said that his heart stopped. I said everybody's heart stops when they die, but for them, the case, if there ever was one, is closed.

The police are in on it, says my son. I knew it.

As much as more work means they're in on it, because they want to avoid work, yes, my father says, they're in on it.

The cops had programs where you could just come and take a syringe, says my son. I thought it was free advertising, myself.

I look at him like the stranger he is. Do those burned boys go to SACK? How many of those boys does Aphra know?

Hey, they're in high school, says my son. High school.

I stir what I thought was going to be dinner.

The syringe is Aphra's, I say. She's doing drugs and dealing to the boys who used to bug my brother, who tried to stop her. These are mostly rich kids, after all, much richer than us. They could afford drugs and the lawyers who tried to do me in with regard to the burning dog. They probably had drugs in the car they were hiding. I remember a couple of them staggering around weirdly after the fire. Although—of course—that could have been from the burning.

Duh, says my son. But quick, stylishly, not like my brother. Get a life, he says.

Suck that back in, says my father. Get a life, he repeats to mock him, even worse, deadpan, perfectly dead.

I turn back to my pot. What life I do have? I dress in the a.m. with the alarm clock my only admirer, I eat what I eat first thing because otherwise I'll have to eat it later and make it for everyone, I lock the door as if hearing the bolt slid is what I go to bed for. Not much, but that's it at the moment, myself alone after a divorce, only recently absolved of burning boys, a woman whose adolescent is in jeopardy on account of her dead brother's girlfriend, after said brother's sudden death.

Sudden and death, both words together, and it's as if the language compresses them into one lead weight, dead and sudden, whizzing straight down.

This syringe makes his death seem less sudden and unknowable, more like someone had thought about it. Even if it is only to deliver a bubble into a vein, the syringe has to be located, the vial has to be raised, the skin must endure puncture. There is time. Time dilutes the sudden.

My son and my father drift to their screens, to watch real cops find syringes, leaving me thinking: no punctures? Nobody looked for punctures.

If only I hadn't shunned my brother. If only I'd insisted my friends pay attention to him. Did I lord over him? That is hard to tell, since I occupied the lording-over point of view as the elder. My brother was an alien to me with his spells—he went somewhere else when his eyes rolled back. If only I weren't so embarrassed about that. If only I were instead just a little bit compassionate, but I stepped back in shock every time, I let somebody else deal with the thrashing and talking. He had good reason to make those Indian burns, but maybe the disease made him do it, or his pills.

I slide the syringe and its bag back into the drawer.

I still see my brother gray-white in the dust storm, struggling to get back from wherever he's gone, wherever he didn't want to go, an electrical storm from his body that would zap me if I touched him, the dust swirling, the storm inside him that couldn't be the true cause of death, too benign, something he carried every day within himself.

Aphra touched him.

Something is boiling that shouldn't be. I turn it down.

If I knew that my brother died "for a reason," so to speak, then I could trust my son to find his own reason, rather than be cursed with his uncle's death by *whatever that was.* If I knew for sure how he died, then I could stop worrying about letting my son go, and find a place for myself. As it stands now, my son will graduate from here but hopefully not be sucked down into the meteor hole of no or little employment that the place offers afterward or try for a disability and its government subsidy that his new friends—let alone the Shove-It boys—talk over. Just as entropy becomes some, it seduces others.

There is college.

I have to go to a SACK meeting and sort things out. But wouldn't my attendance impugn both my father and brother? My father, for all his faults, didn't have the sexually abusing one, and I left my brother at home before his rage turned from annoyance at my mere presence into hatred of someone who had experienced the best result of sex, the biggest payoff of the body, a son of her own. Or else Aphra came along at just the right time. Either way, cheerleaders-turned-tellers watch the parking lots of places like SACK and then talk. They will tell anyone anything while they are giving out money at the bank or change at the grocery store they are so hungry to examine your day of sliding bolts, dressing, and eating. They will talk if I go—they will impugn.

I divide portions of what dinner is cooked, pour water into glasses, find forks and knives.

Going to SACK is not possible. Plexiglass bricks as a wall around my person would sum up how easy it would be to talk to those boys at a meeting like that. But there is glass that can shatter, bricks you could break down. In my youth, I Girl Scouted, I presided over the underachievers in Junior Achievement, I car-washed for cash that saved babies in Africa.

I'll tell you what, I tell the two of them when they're seated. Let's put on a fundraiser for SACK.

Luckily, the county prosecutor finishes with the bone testing fast, or nobody would help me organize the fundraiser. In the end, he doesn't come around to show me the lab report on the dog but just sends me a paper that has the signatures of the judge weighing the bottom half, which closes the books on me. I am declared as innocent as they think anybody who has left here for elsewhere can be, and even though such mail is discrete and private, everyone seems to already know and will answer my call.

I celebrate by taking a walk. I now feel trapped in the car all the time and believe that wanting a walk is progress. It still keeps me secluded. Nobody in this small town gets out of their car unless it is to enter or leave the house. Maybe if walking were forbidden, people would do it, sneaking out at midnight, but otherwise, driving is a sign of wealth—*I don't have to walk even these two blocks to work.* My mother used to take the car out of the carport and park across the street if her bridge club met at the house on the corner.

My son is learning to drive.

Walking makes me feel free, and that's what innocent is. Free, free, free, and getting away with something just to prove my innocence is a particularly twisted free. Moving on my own throws off any guilt I might have about that freedom. I walk past where my brother once crashed his bike, trying to run me over. He lay there with bloodied knees and a scraped cheek, and I ran all the way home to tell on him.

I turn in front of the school, which will let out in fifteen minutes. My son would be embarrassed if I were to be seen anywhere in the school's vicinity. Being seen there would make others wonder if I were being called in to talk with some school authority, so I am practically running when I notice her car parked in the alley where I went through the trash for the dog bones.

What is she doing there?

25

Nice day, I say out the window. Need a lift?

No, thanks anyway, his sister says back. She walks even faster, smiling, pretending she was happy to see me.

I could teach her a thing or two about pretending. What is she doing walking anyway? Thinks she can prove she's better than me by exercise, This is how I stay thin and you don't. *I get angry, very angry. I start the car. How dare she. She looks like a walking piece of celery. Then I'm sad and insulted. What does she know about sadness? Some sad people can't eat; some eat their heart out and then double desserts. But her? I don't think she's sad either way. She never cared nothing about him. She's just trying to replace him in the family now, hanging around here all this long time.*

I want to run her over.

A blast from the radio calms me: cattle prices. I think about cattle prices. The poor cattle going to slaughter. I start to cry and turn off Sport. I have to focus. The kids are coming out. One of them will be him. I turn Sport back on and drive closer. He walks like his uncle, his arms down like that, the way he stops short at the corner.

I could be the school guard, moving kids along after they leave. But I'm not.

26

I invite the whole town to raise SACK funds. In exchange, *Do you buy drugs from Aphra?* is the question I want answered from its members, who'll be the big benefiters. Of course, the Shove-It boys would never answer such a question. But what happens on the premises can be assessed, and that could count for something. Besides, girls will show at a fundraiser in a town of this size, and girls make boys their age liable to spark and smoke and do anything.

The ghostly season is upon us, the excuse for as impersonal a fundraiser as you can throw, a costume party. The boys can all come as dealers—what do you think? I say.

Mom, my son says.

We purchase paper plates and gut pumpkin, lard the larder, and consider bodyguards. They are called chaperones, my son says.

They are people who disappear with their own agendas, says my father. Maybe somebody will like your mother. Fundraisers aren't all about the money.

He winks. But he doesn't really want me with someone, or else I'd defrost somewhere else and run a dishwasher that isn't his own. He plans to come as a grandfather.

You can tell, he tells us, by the glued-on grasshopper affixed to my baseball cap. It has hopped already.

A costume is supposed to be an alter ego, I complain.

Grandfathers need their egos altered? he says, pulling at his face folds underneath. Other things altered, maybe. He gives me his most charming squint and lets me laugh.

He could derail this, he reminds me, with all his cute talk.

The chaperones, chaperoned by their own wives or husbands, come wearing mostly costumes from space epics, since all the town's stores have them in clearance. I hardly know any of them now after years away and less than a year back, and certainly not in costume. For my part, I am not so much a woman without a husband as a sister without a brother to those few who know me now. I come as a cop, in a blue suit, with a star and a club, not exactly suggestive, except to my son. But my attorney nods in approval and shakes hands with someone dressed as a space cowboy. Wonderful thing, her saving those boys' lives, says the attorney.

I tap my club and smile.

My son has died over and over, having to invite anyone his age at all. Then they actually turn up. The girls show, all rosy where their costumes expose them to the cool weather. The boys favor masks that cover their whole heads, the adolescent solution to social terror. At first, the masks are an identification problem. It is only by fashion labels on jeans or T-shirts that I can make out which boy is which. But rubber at the neck quickly bottles up the head heat, and soon the masks are shucked, soon these unmasked boys and girls stand on the deck in the late light, avoiding and attracting each other, soon they are up to no good.

We leave them alone, as we must. At least I appear to be leaving them alone. I hand over the small checks of contribution to the Boy Scout leader who runs SACK, along with the secondhand sewing machines a few bring, assorted used board games, mismatched cutlery, and a cutting board, all of which appear on SACK's wish list. The leader also runs the radio station, so there's been good publicity. He's wearing his khakis, and his wife is Mrs. BoPeep, with a crook. They radiate a godliness that's creepy and leave the center open on weekends unsupervised, *such good kids!*

We withdraw to the front room to drink scotch my father has made a good horror gray with drops from three food colorings, and we watch a televised event, not quite a movie, with stars and bad music so that we can talk or not to whomever stands beside us, glass in hand, eyes averted. But not quite all of us withdraw to the scotch and all that faux talk. A guy wearing a T-shirt that says *Costume*, which shows off his broad shoulders, helps me pull on one of the discarded heads. I've put down my club but can't get the head to fit. He has to screw it on, the neck part is so rubbery. My hair gets caught and has to be fooled with. He's gentle. He says his wife had hair like mine.

Had.

I go all jelly and flee into the dark the back deck has become. I stand around in my head and hide the star of my cop outfit under a sweater and remember the feeling of the man's fingers at the soft of my neck. Is there someone in this town who could imagine me other than someone's mother or daughter?

Maybe he's partial to police.

Just then fireworks blow, saved from my son's summer haul—such a saver! I am jolted back to the party and its celebration of evil and sexuality, minus the abuse, by the giggles after the explosions from the clumps around the boom box, clumps of kids chasing other clumps.

I can't tell who's burned in this light so smoky from the blown fireworks. My son says they have given up their grill-fronted car and now come to school in a hearse and wear hoods and call themselves the Hoods. They must have jettisoned their hoods tonight in favor of something else, maybe themselves on such a scary night, since so many wear scars, press-on or otherwise, so many have that jettisoned *Who am I?* hood-look.

And others are still coming. Cars slam shut from their spots on the street, figures fly over the lawn. I would say more than twenty of them are milling around.

Dear, I say to my son, whose shoes give him away, and he dodges me for more food. I'm keeping my eyes open, I say to his back.

He turns around and glares at me from inside his own head, as he should for such a straight, no-way-around-it statement. I let him go, seared by his glance, but keep a close watch on the rest disembarking their cars and what they get to doing.

A moth settles on the lawn in the midst of them, a large gray moth in the fireworks' smoke, with coat hangers for feelers. She—surely it is a female and Aphra, since no one else could be that size moth—glides in under the trees, feelers bobbing, to where shelter would be if all the leaves weren't off. Like a production from Shakespeare, she becomes part of a play, the bare trees framing the stage that is the lawn, the distance between her and them and me artificial in the leftover light, with the chorus of the almost grown. Aphra moves across the lawn in a slow half circle, as if dazed to be there, fresh hatched in her wings. She doesn't have to move closer—a few figures separate from the others and approach her.

I watch from the deck, my breath held.

Aphra folds herself. Those few moving rush her anyway, make her scoot her small but heavily laden feet into the last bit of light. But they don't chase her off the way we did when their ages were ours, when the very fathers of these boys taunted her, would run after her to touch her and shove her in a way they did no other girl, and then leave her for my brother.

The boys want something else now. They rush her and touch her. She turns toward them as if she has something for them, and they rush her again. Her feelers go all abob. Then, like their forebears, the boys turn away from her for good, walking into the dusk as smoothly as dusk takes the lawn, the light stolen, Aphra forgotten. Her hands go up in that dusk, palms out, as startled a signal as a real moth might make, one just singed.

I duck inside. The cider is almost ready. I stir together an unnatural mix of Chex and Tabasco sauce. I empty Black Cats into bowls and align all the Cracker Jack boxes we haven't yet given to rogue children who ring our bell and present us with bags despite the rubber-spidered knob and the webbed porch light hung with chicken bone, and whatever else my son has exhumed from the kitchen discards, as well as ectoplasm that moans from a package he has wired under the welcome mat.

Welcome, Aphra is what I think, stirring the crunch mix. Welcome, for filling this chink in my big *What is going on?* Now I will stroll across the lawn and say, Game's up—give me the cash you've just taken for the drugs. Confess at least this. My heart exercises itself furiously at such a clever trap as mine, but then Aphra comes in on her own, covered in donkey tails.

I thought they were just playing tag, she whimpers, and I was it. But they stuck these all over me, even where I can't see—she hunches her shoulders forward to show how she can't see past her breasts.

It looks like part of the costume, I say. Very theatrical. The tails add to it.

She stops tearing them off. She gives me a smile that reads, *You're crazy.*

I pour a gray scotch for her in no celebration, my question unanswered, my lead lost. I pour my own.

In a small town, you have to swallow.

She drinks her scotch fast, a way of quaffing that is more consuming than drinking. Where's your son? she asks, pouring herself a second. I haven't seen him yet.

If I don't say, she'll find him anyway. Second Darth Vader on your left, I lie. Or he could be the third. I can't help but notice the man in the *Costume* T-shirt talking to a short witch.

Aphra goes coy as she cuts a swath down the line of drunken Darths, endangering every one of them with her feelers as she plucks off the last taped tails. Pardon me, she says, while she sticks them to the blind sides of the Darth breathing boxes.

My brother's house she has entered and entered, I'm sure of that—but not the house where he grew up, not here, and not even for his wake. My brother was never a great inviter in his youth, and she harbors streaks of shyness the way bacon is streaked, between boldnesses. Sure, she is upset by the tail game, but that isn't what has drawn her inside now. Less humiliation lay in returning to her car and driving off. I think she's here because she feels entitled, like a widow. She's a merry widow on the make, and I want to signal to my son—who is where?—to lie low. After all, she's my number one murder suspect. She finally plants herself—feelers awry and wings spread—beside the last Darth, a big one, and downs her drink.

A gorilla wearing my son's shoes emerges from the outside dark. He wants the popcorn balls for his friends outside, balls he manufactured all weekend, each stuck with a soft pink already-chewed-looking gum in the middle that I told him is not the best center for such a ball, that people will be disgusted when they bite into it and throw it down. I put them out of sight, hoping he wouldn't ask.

May the farts be with you, says my gorilla, worming his way through all the epic costumes. I'm waving *Other way! Other way!* but he ignores me as a young man might his mother, slides the box of balls out from under the pushed-back chair beside Aphra, and hoists it to his shoulder. Aphra turns her feelers toward him as he lifts and exposes his armpit, although clothed. She sniffs and says loud in her *Please* voice, Can I help you?

This undoes my son. The box waggles as the armpits struggle to close off their odor, and in his throes, popcorn balls leap from the box. They fall all over the place.

Are we supposed to bob for them? shouts my father, himself scotch-lit. He levers down to his knees to bite at one that has landed at his feet, with his hands behind his back. No one says, *That's apples*—they stop talking and dodge the stickiness. Other balls attach to their Wookie wigs and a few heirloom settlers' costumes, including Aunt Fay's jodhpurs, and one gutters a candle in a pumpkin that sends up a flare.

There's enough smoke for the alarm in seconds.

Okay, party's over, I say into the din, jerking the alarm from the wall. Oh, I say something more polite, but that's the gist of it. My son flees quickly with his new friends to ring doorbells or to use foam unnaturally or what I can't now blame on Aphra. They load their hearses and cars with toilet paper and whatever of the fireworks are left and squeal off in the stench of burned rubber, while their parents and the Boy Scout couple move slowly to my door, still chatting despite the alarm, swallowing the dregs of their now very gray scotch. Aphra makes for the door too, her wings collecting any last balls off the side tables where I have stowed them. When I pass her, wielding my sticky broom, she clutches at the handle. Wasn't the gorilla with the balls the one you meant?

I make a laugh like such a mix-up is the point of such a party, which it is when you can control it. He must have switched heads, I say. Other friends were looking for him.

Friends, I say twice.

It is a low blow, but I could have said, *Leave him alone!*

She frowns and releases the broom. She seems sure the real point of a party is to point and prod at her, but she's not always sure about how or when or whether. I guess, she says. She sheds a few more leftover balls in her flounce toward the door.

I douse the few fiery ones the kids lit on the way out, sprinkling them with gray diluted punch. All the rest of the two dozen my son made and chewed, I shove into the trash can, and I am peeling the chewed centers off its plastic cover when I wave at the man in the *Costume* T-shirt shaking hands with my father, thanking him for the party. He leaves with the witch.

Loved the finale, says my father, enjoying himself, smiling as wide as the curve of his glass, still sporting his glued-on grasshopper cap. He's almost up to washing the punch bowl, but he's still experimenting with more colors, he says, testing an idea he has about psychology and color and drinking.

I rinse cups, and then I sweep up the balls. I sweep toward the protoplasm and the web surrounding the door, where I find Aphra, crying on the step with a box in her arms.

That came today, I say. They've finally started forwarding his mail.

I've been picking it up, she says. At least these boxes. She sobs, and then she says something that starts the same as her name: *Aphrodisiac of the Month.*

Now that is sad. But she doesn't stay long enough for me to express whatever I can. Flustered or not, she goes back out into the dark, feelers first.

My son I find an hour later, already back in his room.

Aphra ruined my party, he says. Rising wearily from his computer, he takes long, proud steps over to his bed and collapses onto it.

I tell him pheromones are free—I can't keep her from sniffing.

No one, he says, punching his pillow, not even my uncle, would have had anything to do with someone like that. You saw how she was. You saw the tails they stuck to her. Was that a drug thing?

Maybe it was, I say. I can't figure her out.

He smolders. He's too old to hug without his recoiling. I pick up his loose head instead and put it under my arm for storage. I crumple candy wrappers into a ball and say, *Two points*, when I hit the overflowing trash.

He's still quiet.

I'm sorry, I say. I'll do something. Don't worry.

Staring at the orange flame of the pumpkin on his windowsill, I see my son small and Aphra so large. I see he's new to how some women are lost—he's young despite all his old talk. There, by the light of the guttering pumpkin, I see his face less angry, more afraid.

27

Mom says, Get over him, he's dead.

I could throw my damn butterfly costume at her. I don't. I hang it in the closet.

Mom doesn't notice. She only notices what she has to. When Dad used to get angry, she hid in the bathroom, never noticing me. I would have hid in the bathroom too, except for all the leaks in there. On a rainy day, you could take a shower without even turning it on. It got so we put the shower curtain up along the ceiling, it was so wet. She said those were her tears coming down the side of the wall. Her saying that just made me angry, even when I was little and confused. We had a door that opened—even the bathroom door opened—and she could have walked away from him and taken me with her. At least that's what they were always telling her at that restaurant she worked at. That's where we once had to sleep in a booth all night.

That's true—he's dead, I say.

When I look up from the hole I have been boring into the closet wall with my not-sharp nail, she says, You have to move on.

I look back into the closet. Am I looking for something? Like a dad? I'm the one who always said to people my dad died early. After he abused me so much people noticed and he got put away, there we still were, with a wet ceiling. I never got pregnant. I think that's because I was heavy already and whatever seeds got lost inside me and rotted.

Move to where? I can't move, I say slowly. I can hardly make half the rent here.

A Quickee Mart is opening on the highway, says Mom, and I see her hand coming around to finger my costume that she knows is too small for her. No more beds. You'll soon make plenty, she says. And think of all those candy bars you can sneak for yourself. She sighs. You're just too darn depressed to have around is all. She picks up some of the stuff she herself threw to the floor. I'm going to have a live-in boyfriend, and I don't want you to ruin it.

Mom—

I'll give you a month.

I leave the bedroom and go stand in the pantry, getting the door almost completely shut. I see we've used up almost all the toilet paper. Then I go to sit in Sport for a while. Sport, I say. It's cold in here.

I drive around, burn gas, and park behind the railroad loading area. Trains don't stop here anymore. They rush by in the middle of the night, real noisy and filled with coal. When I was in high school and couldn't go home because Mom had some other boyfriend, this is where I would stay. Nobody even goes here to kiss. It's a little harder to hide with a car, but it's dark now. I fool with my phone. Here I know I'll sleep happy, my head against his shirt, the one I stretched over the seat.

28

The Boy Scout and Bo-Peep run off with all the funds from the fundraiser and skip town. At least they only took money and a few keyboards and whatever chalk the funders could spare is what I hear from those who donated. No one says I set them up—though I put the whole fundraiser thing in motion with my house as the location. But no one comes around asking me to put together a bake sale after; no committee knocks at my door with a really good idea. I'm persona non grata yet again.

I tried.

I go back to sorting my brother's mess of papers, and to my surprise, two boxes in, I find a letter my brother wrote from college:

Dear Mother, he writes, *I am sorry that I can't come home during the five-day break. I don't have enough money for the bus, and I need more for next semester. My hands are almost healed from the electric burn, and they say I can have my job back at the canteen, an opportunity I don't think I can refuse.*

I hope to have money for the bus by the end of the term. It's only two hundred miles, but that's too far to walk.

His handwriting spools out in such hopeful loops. Is that what a bully sounds like when he gets older and leaves home and is poor? Or is that how an electrocution survivor sends a message to try to get his mother to help him? I check the date: it wasn't a month after being let out of the motel. He must still have had bandages on at least his back, if not his "almost healed" hands. Why didn't they send him money for the bus? Why didn't they pick him up?

It will make you strong, was always my father's excuse. I don't know what my mother's excuse was. Lack of mothering skill, or self-pity? Why was I chosen to have a child with seizures, a clumsy child who hurt himself? Why won't he grow up enough so I'm not responsible anymore, so I don't have to bother with him? They must have decided that he was old enough to cope with the aftermath of the electrocution totally by himself. He took a bus to the first day of classes, and they never visited.

Not that they visited me. But I thought that's because they were busy with him.

Then I discover that my brother didn't pick up boards in that town he went to for a while. I don't think he ever worked there. Maybe he never even saw the place. What I find, buried in a wad of receipts, is a discharge. Not a snot-on-a-rag discharge, but the military's. A medical discharge, of course. He enlisted that year in a war that wasn't for winning but was conjured up to be seen for its glory and oil revenues. *O say can you see?* was how the TV put it. A sort of political tour group was probably how he saw it, with someone to say *Get up* in the a.m. and *Here's dinner* when it got dark, kind of like a tour to South America because the Mexicans from here matched those to be killed. But it wasn't Mexico where he made this tour of duty—it was the Gulf, which explains why he was so tanned when he returned from being away.

Too many spells, reads the discharge. A photo folded inside it shows him standing in front of a tower of boxes about two men high. He's smiling and half-covering the symbol and the letters "DU."

Even I know what that stands for: depleted uranium. My father shakes his head after I hand him the snapshot at lunch. I never moved boxes like that, he says, turning over the photo. You have to be stupid to do something like that.

He wanted to be a hero, I say.

My father replaces the photo in the fold of the discharge. They didn't have ammunition like that when I went to war—that stuff's radioactive, he says. I read about it in the papers. They said the military recycles the casings after they shoot them. Then they're sent back to the States in crates like that one. No one told personnel to wear gloves or protective coverings.

That would make a person get sick and die.

He didn't sicken and die, says my father.

My father didn't do anything heroic either, except feed stray dogs in the Philippines where he was a cook.

I shuffle through the wadded receipts, in case anything else falls out. All I remember, I say, was that he said birds drove him away from that town of boards we now know he made up, birds that he wanted to fly around free, uncaged, that could tell people when to get out.

Canaries, says my father. Sick canaries. All the birds have some radioactivity now in their bones.

Like people?

He pulls out his lighter and flicks it. Your brother's dead, he says, and leans down and lights my brother's discharge. I don't want your mother to find this.

But that's his, I shout. That's all we have. I grab what's left of the paper and smother its fire. I take it back, singed and all, and tuck it in with the receipts, with the coupons, all the little litter of his life now, kept in a shoebox under the bronco creamer.

29

The Quickee Mart has a new policy, one that isn't on the application, says the boss. We only want help that can run during holdups. Let's see you run.

I glare at him. Thank you, I say, because that's all you can do after someone says something like that.

He clears his throat.

I leave the application on the counter, half-filled out.

He doesn't look up.

30

We are a normal family.

That's what my mother says getting off the train to her seatmate from Chicago, the town that dries her out now and then, and especially post–dead son. Such an embarrassment. She only comes back when everything in the family is really normal.

It was a wet spring when I left, is what we hear after she says goodbye to the seatmate when she sees all of us standing in the terminal, and we know what she means. Liquor running in the gutters, blocking crosswalks, streaming down street signs until the warnings were hard to read, until it was not just bad eyesight at stake. Sometimes she saw it dry the way we hoped she would, but she had her preferences, her style of self-revelation. And shortly after my brother died, she went over a cataract.

My son takes her bag. It's bigger than a handbag but smaller than luggage. He unloads it from her scrawny arm.

Not so fast, she says. There's a gun in there. I've got a gun.

We freeze.

She fishes a gun made of wax out of her bag. A wick sticks out of its barrel and it flops around when she waves it. It's the sort of thing you can't take on a plane, she says. But perfect for trains.

We are a normal family. My father doesn't talk about aliens to just anybody—they have to bring it up. My dead brother hangs out in the middle of nowhere with a shovel. I artfully place dog bones around pastures at night as a hobby. And my son never raises his armpits to anyone.

Nice, says my son. Nice gun.

We are intergenerationally normal.

She doesn't give him the gun. Instead, she hauls out the rest of her presents right there on the train platform: a wax screwdriver for me for my loose screws, a wax Tastykake for my father, who only eats the waxy icing anyway, and a reproduction, also in wax, of St. Sebastian, with all the arrows sticking out, for my son. A casting problem, she says, a very tricky mold. I worked a lot in wax this time.

Every family is this normal. They try not to let on how normal unless someone needs a wax gun, and then you make excuses, make it normal to have one, in case of a holdup in a church. Whoever noticed my brother, with a family as normal as this?

My father has all his smokers—some of them ordered from a catalog and assembled, some, like the TV, in the process of disassembling—going full out in the backyard when she arrives. It could be the gates of hell or the past on TV that you look out on from the bay window that juts into the smoke, the bay window like some sci-fi vehicle aimed for the center of the earth, where it's always molten.

Have the neighbors complained? she asks while we stare out that bay window, caught in the smoke and the suspense of her return.

Less and less, my father says. They give me fish and I return them smoked and tasty straight from the TV.

I believe this smoking you are doing has replaced me, she says, taking a seat where she can't see it.

No, no, he says, pointing at a chair for me. It was just before he died that I got the kit, he says. Then you left. I started before. Not after.

She falls so silent in that confusion of time that I don't sit down. I should be getting ice cubes anyway or at least uncorking. She starts rising from her own seat, as if she will pour, a disorientation of hers that always lasts long past her drying out. But I don't mind her getting up like that—it's almost motherly. I am glad she has all her words, that her slur is no worse, that she is not too sad.

Don't explain your smoke to me, she says. This is a ritual, like church, she says, waving her hands toward it. This is a ritual like the way the pills they bring me ritually purify. The way they—reduce.

She touches her toes. She tells everyone who asks that she goes away to Chicago to reduce. Not that she reduces. She is always thin, her toes never far off. Your brother could do two hundred of these, she says, touching her toes. Literally two hundred.

He was normal, I say. He could have been a long liver.

Children always kill their parents so they can live, says my mother. Anyway, that's what they're supposed to do.

I wish we were all about to cry. Instead, we pretend to be normal, except for a great fat tear behind my father's glasses, which could be just the result of all the smoke he has just come in from.

Don't make it so hard, says my father, surprising me.

Hard is what we are made of, says my mother, centuries of hard ice and scotch and soda. Did you fix the ice maker? she asks. She's at the freezer now, its white smoke pouring out over her hands.

The repairman was here yesterday, my father sighs.

Weeks of ice and fire flowed through my mother after my brother died. She drank so much I decided she must have been the one to kill him, with guilt like that, and so she deserved to drink like that. Guilt compounded over years of indifference is hard to solace. Before she took her train to Chicago, she took time off for good behavior—she sang in the choir, jammed hot dogs into buns, caught fish in a stocked lake. But what all that time off did was build up her thirst. Slaking it, she took several weeks more before she could be fooled into going away. How fashionable, we told her; how criminal if not. A car with her at the wheel wanted little for a collision. No driving was the final nail.

People just don't like to walk.

Lots of families send their loved ones to dry out, and they're normal, we told her.

That's always what they like to tell you, she answered, kicking at a packed hatbox.

She wants to drink to his death now. A toast in remembrance. We all know she could drink right up to the anniversary, right through it. We hem and haw like it is a country dance we're involved in, just a matter of swinging in the right place. Then she wrenches the ice tray free from the freezer, twists it in a crash to break the quiet.

There's only schnapps, she says with a sigh, closing a sideboard door. Everything else seems to be finished.

Hidden, no one says.

This no-liquor-in-the-house situation raises the shopping flag, the let's-go-buy-lots idea. While I fool around collecting stray cubes, my father says, Those smokers sure are smoking.

We flatly refuse shopping.

Then my father says, I don't want to bury anyone else ever.

My mother doesn't even turn to face him.

I want to go first, he goes on. It's only fair. I'm the oldest.

With your hardy stock, you'll have to off yourself, says my mother. She walks over to her bag and produces six tiny airline vials of whiskey. Only they're a little bigger—they're train size, she says. I also made a wax whiskey bottle, but empty, she says with sadness. You see why I didn't want you to have my bag? she says to my son. Occupational therapy, she cheerfully announces. Find me a glass.

Where's my son? she asks after two. My son, she says. Where is he?

I can drive you over to see his stone, I say. They put it up last week.

She shakes her head, unscrewing her third.

You mean me? says my son.

She looks at him like he is part of a color blur on a channel she only just tuned in to and means to change soon with the remote. She lifts her free hand as if she will—he's not quite right—and says, No.

My father doesn't tell her about aliens or about the boxes of shells her son moved during a war that she watched on TV. She doesn't really want to know why he's not here—she's not stupid. She's had time to think about him and the whatever that took him away. She covers her ice with more scotch.

It's a conspiracy, you see, she says, lifting her glass. There's more than one person involved. That's why we don't know where he is. First the doctors say where he is, then the church, then the funeral people—but that's all made up. She drinks. You've got to go find him for yourself, she says. Those hazy days just after, when he was lying around in his rouge and with real preservatives running through him and not this stuff—she cracks the seal on her fourth small bottle—I looked for him. It's like those people who listen when somebody says You're dead, and then they are. All the atoms get together and believe. Although I ask you all like a polite person where he is, I already know where he is, the alive one—he's wherever I believe he is, not where they say.

She looks at us as if we don't believe her, and then she swigs the whole of the last bottle down straight.

31

That woman is back, says Mom.

She means his mom. Mom always thought I should have done better. He's a sort of cripple, she used to say. And besides, what did his mom do but drink? I could've done that.

She forgets that she did, for quite a while.

It's a big responsibility being the only son, is what he always said about his mom. The burden is great, but so are the rewards.

I looked around for the rewards. Not such a great house, and you're working for your dad.

I give my mom stock market tips, and she follows them, he said. Her investment club is very impressed.

This was when he was at the motel with his stinking burns. I would peel off the bandages and reapply fresh ones with antibiotic. The nurse taught me how. I saved him quite a bit of money by helping out. He thanked me, and I said, Stop that.

Even after getting over his burns in that motel, he would call his mother on the phone every day to ask about something he saw on TV. Did she think the president should not have declared the fighting over, which general needed better advice, what did the price of oil mean? She would answer his questions out of her TV watching, and that made him happy, because he watched the same programs. Except he knew more than she did—he'd actually been there. Don't criticize the cook, he'd say if I ever said anything.

As for his sister, he said she got the nurses going at the hospital while he was out to lunch. If she hadn't, I don't know what would have happened, he said. She's really something.

32

You're nothing but a nothing,
You're not a thing at all

went the song from inside the record player that took a thick disk the size of a personal pizza that turned around and around, lazily, afternoon on afternoon, under an old-time needle.

My brother's favorite song. He would snatch up the LP and sing along without the music—and then we'd all sing along. By being born, we made a nothing out of my mother—she told us often she wanted to be an artist. By our being born, my mother could never be anything other than the small-town kind of nothing, and if my arrival didn't nail that nothing on the head, my brother's flattened it. What she gave us in return was this record so we would not forget the nothing we made of her and her artistry.

She is good at wax guns.

People will always say children are stupid, that they lack knowledge or experience, but not that they are nothing. Usually, a child is an addition, a something, more help at least.

I'm still humming the song. That record player needle went deep into my groove—it took at least a decade before the record, thick as it was, encountered the trouble of truth. I'm humming along while hanging a black shirt on the line I use at the grain elevator to get the housework over with during the day in my lunch hour, snapping clothespins onto the shoulders of that shirt.

Boys wear black like women now. It makes them nothing in the night. An arm can come up and brush a girl's bra without any prior sign of an arm. My son wears his black shirt to stand at the edge of dark dances and watch. He's still girl-shy.

Maybe he brushes.

To wear this black shirt makes him something. Not exactly the something of happiness, but not the death of it. This is one thing we agree on. He doesn't agree on the idea of *If this, then this* much yet. That is, it's all *What about me?* first. I have to get my something first, or else it's *Is my shirt dry?*

At least the shirt won't freeze out here. It's been such a warm fall, and the sun is out.

My brother took our mother's nothing and put it on, because she gave it to him. Oh, she gave him other things, along the line of wax guns, most like: *Hold this* or *I don't know why I carried this out of the store. Please put it somewhere.* Or in my case, *It looked good on the rack, but now I see the color just isn't me.* My brother would snap and claw for these discards as if they were food falling from a great height down, down, down to his great depth. He would take the whatever with the snap of a bottom feeder. Me? I swam to the top with whatever nothing I was given, to see, in the bright sunshine, what a nothing it was.

My brother took my mother's nothing and put it on like a shirt, and it was rarely what everyone else was wearing. My mother didn't care about what anyone else thought, so he didn't either. I dragged my nothing out of this primordial water and tried to turn it inside out, into a something, without knowing that this kind of nothing is the black hole kind, one that doesn't invert, that sucks in any something you make along with it. Hence, I found my ex and I now help out at the elevator.

But I have hope, and my son, who has nothing to do with nothing, unless everyone else does. Though, I understand this is just a phase. Already he shows signs that he doesn't quite get this song of my mother's. Look at how he drives—that's something!

At least my mother, in her indifference, never babysat. Nothingness like that is highly contagious. And that nothing record she bought is finally broken, or else the player no longer works. Not that my father broke it. He went along with that record. A father is something until a son comes along and says he's nothing. Fathers want to prevent that. They can't, but they often try hard—it's instinct. Not that my father had to try too hard with my brother. But it's not all instinct with my mother. After all, she bought the record.

I can't stop humming the song even after I go back inside.

I'm humming away, staring at the top of those elevators where nonmigrating or confused or adapted birds tip and look into the window at me looking at them, and even a few clouds parade by—a few crocodiles in the fluff or rabbit triplet cumulus on account of the weather, a sailor's delight—until, over my hum, the men around the elevator start shouting, filling trucks with corn they've sold at last: Pull up another foot! Whoa there! and what do you know, my brother comes to visit, no swoop of dust and a shovel or even haze set down on my desk—he's here.

I stop my hum.

He's in the trim on the door, and I am happy for him. Whatever it takes to give off such a presence as would hold him in that trim is good. He could have come into the wall calendar of big green vehicles hung a foot over, but that would have been too flashy. Nothing about those thin flat trim boards painted in a color other than the walls lends mystery or even surprise to him squeezing himself into them in that everywhere way of the dead. But what exactly is he doing spread out on my trim in this bird- and cloud- and shout-filled day?

What? He wants my shoes? We do wear the same size, if not style, even if he is a smidgen longer in the toes—and we're exactly the same if I'm in my short heels, which I am not. I have unlaced and kicked off running shoes, ones that, unlike the heels, he could indeed wear, that he had worn more than once in our youth, sneaking his feet into their kicked-off selves while I was not looking, like now, and running off. I sort through the space under my desk with my feet and hook one shoe on, and then the back end of the other slips away. I search around fast with my toes of my unshod foot so I can get over to the trim he is in, in time.

It's not his actual self, mind you, that flutters on that trim but just the same feeling that I had in the dust storm around that figure, though this time there's just feeling and no him. Then that feeling shifts.

Maybe it's me, struggling to scoot into my shoes, or maybe it's the way he must be moving them to confuse me, but I can't get them on and get over there in time. I could bend over and catch the shoes in my hands, but then I would lose sight of the trim and maybe all this trim feeling of him. What does he want that he gets me in such a hurry for my shoes anyway? Has he come to retrieve his shovel? Of course. He wants everything, the shovel, the shoes, the keyboard, my pumping heart, all the stuff you leave behind when you're in his condition—that is, dead. But I don't say that out loud, and I try not to even think it, because I don't want him to get depressed and leave. If he wants my shoes instead of the shovel, maybe that's a good sign. I don't know—it's something different from being dead.

We don't actually exchange words while I'm fooling around, not even on my part. I always kept my face looking away when we spoke before anyway. Maybe I pretended he was dead. I didn't speak then for the same reason I don't now: people will see me speaking to him. Now farmers would walk in and catch me at it, wanting their slips and toppling into my office as they wipe the chaff stuck to their skin and eyebrows, and I would be smack in the way, talking to the door trim.

But what he wants is changing. The whole time, I am tense, trying to get specific about this, and by now I'm standing in the middle of the room in one shoe, the other in my hand, wondering whether to heave it. Is it like when my son stands a little too close and, being far too tall for his age, can't help but look down my décolleté while he asks for money but what he really wants instead is for me to look up at him and take notice? No. My brother has had my attention better now dead than when he was alive.

More mystery.

I think my brother is daring me. At first, I think he is daring me to believe that he's in the wall trim, *Come on*, but what he's actually doing is daring me to find out what really happened.

Dare you, he says.

How does he know that I've nearly lost interest, that giving up has been on my mind because the mind moves on? It makes up what it needs. How does he know that, except that he's now in that ineffable aerosol, spirit, one of those bug bombs you set off that gets into everything you touch or breathe?

I walk right over to the door and press my ear to the trim. For sure somebody like Don Marsh, heavyweight champion of three counties, will come through the door with me glued to its side, but I don't care.

Care? Is that what he's saying? As in *Don't care?* Or *Don't dare?* Is that my mind talking or his?

My brother doesn't want my shoes, for sure. I give up—I write down *Care* when I get back to my desk, as if it is a message as clear as *Please call back*. While I'm writing, my toes finally manage to fit into both shoes. They're unlaced, of course, but at least they're on. With both shoes on, I look at my note, and I crumple it.

One blizzard, my brother and I walked back from grade school, heads down, and I lost him, not watching or talking. Snow here can fly horizontal across the land, can sweep and lodge in your throat when you turn around to shout, Hurry it up. I coughed up snow twice in a warm spit, shouting and turning around that day to see that he wasn't dragging himself forward any more behind me. He was gone, and it seemed no more spit or cough of mine would make him show. Circling back as best I could over the sidewalk bumps of snow and same-size shrubs, I couldn't find a single dropped glove of him. How I would get in trouble, coming in without him, it being my job to look after him and pretend not to.

I stood in the cold blowy snow, lifting my feet up and down but not forward toward the door, worrying, worrying, until my father opened that sliding door and looked out past where I was standing and shouted my name so loud I tipped and some of the snow on me fell off. Over here, I barely said, and I made my way through the snow-encrusted door hole as if I were now caught and would be turned right around to look a little farther, when I saw my brother at the table, spoon down in soup, smiling. He had run past me in the snow while I was circling and calling and coughing, and made a big deal out of being first, picking out the first roast beef sandwich for himself to go with the soup. He was now laughing, yes, laughing, when I came in to Where have you been? from my mother, who vied with my father for making us tough so that we didn't bother them. Now I had bothered them, and for my lateness, I was whacked on the bottom.

Don't care? Or *Don't dare?* I can't do the nothing they want me to do.

33

I used to paint the best nails. Rad, very rad. They were like the very ends of me concentrated, really attractive. Not that her brother ever said that, because that would have ignored the rest of me, but he did admire them. I can do backfill, sculpting, shaping, curing, water marbling, glitter, press-ons with smiley faces, and of course fake nails. I mix eye shadow into clear polish and get a black that some people love. I could look all day at my nails after I finish them, look into them like a mirror. That's me? I once did just the tips gold.

I haven't polished them at all since he died. The cuticles are chewed around the stubs. I also stopped taking vitamins for them. Now not even the crummy Studebaker Studio will take me on as a stylist. They considered me before, put me on a list. This time, instead of my chewed nails, they used the excuse that I couldn't fit in the chair. Pull yourself together, said the evil woman in charge. You're still crying all over the place.

Sport, I tell my car, just bed-making will put us out on the street for good. What should we do? I'm out of job ideas and hungry. Should we sneak home to the fridge and see what's inside or open some of the bags of chips as best I can with these poor stubs? Or both? What kind of sad am I today? Where is that son of hers to watch driving around?

You're big because of your glands, said her brother. The way he said glands *made me want more of them.*

34

My son walks into my grain elevator office angry. He wants to call the police.

When I step out into the street, when I walk up the steps to the front of the school, when I play b-ball, Aphra's there. I can't buy a slice without her in my face. It's too much.

The subtext is that he also can't have a girl if this old woman is on him, not that he wants girls, not that he is actually that age, not really. Or else I'm blind to the developmental jump. I'm probably blind. Okay, okay, I say.

She's big, right? he says. She stands in the way so I have to walk around her. My friends think she's creepy, he says. People are tired of her. Me, I'm tired.

I don't tell him my father told me that before my brother went away, he once called the cops on Aphra. He couldn't get rid of her either. Is this a kind of domestic violence? they asked him when they showed up. He didn't know cops laugh at domestic violence when a man calls. It is bad enough, their response, when a woman calls. Besides, they knew about the others who had had Aphra in their youth—the force's own members. My brother thought they were professionals. That woman? they said, like he was no man. So my brother never called the cops again that my father knew of, and after a while, that was that. No other girl would even consider him while Aphra followed him around. There was never a girl after Aphra.

This is serious, my son says.

I nod, I know.

Out the window, two lost dogs are getting lured into a truck that the cops bought not a week ago, a big white four-door with a wire screen attached to the back seat. I don't say to my son, to distract him, *Look*—that's all the work cops do in this small town, dog felonies. I don't remind him that one of them has a Shove-It son, one of the Hoods. I say, I will speak to them about Aphra. But it's you who has to tell her directly to leave you alone—she won't pay attention to anyone else.

No. He fears that what he has to say will come out wrong—not so much that he will hurt her, because he is past that at his age or not up to it, but that his mere act of speaking will open up more talk time for her, as in dialogue.

I suggest a trap for confronting her. Get the one or two guys you know to gather around, and they can say, *Go away*—not you—so she listens. But kindly, I say. Your uncle did die not so long ago. He did spend a lot of his time with her.

He sighs like I am a computer in a brownout, that unreasonable. He shakes his head. She would love the attention. The other day when we were trying to skateboard in the park—

That's it, I say, getting an idea out of the thinnest air, the mystical. My brother himself will tell her she should stop. We'll stage a séance.

My son throws up his hands and walks out.

35

What my own big fear is, I can't tell anybody about. It's hard to carry this big a fear inside a person. It's been growing like the tumor Mom had for a year that was first just a bump and then a baseball, and then they cut it off her like she had an extra arm. My fear is baseball-sized. I wonder why everybody can't see it. I think my face shows it. I look in the mirror a lot these days, because I don't look at my nails anymore, and there are pinched parts around my mouth when I put on lipstick.

Lipstick on a pig? They can go to hell.

If I have to make myself look ridiculous again to force them to notice and get an answer to my big fear, so be it. I'm not afraid of people laughing at me—they do that just seeing my size anyway. I laugh at that fear. Nobody like her brother is going to see past my size and sweep me off my feet again, which he really did. To show off how strong he was, he carried me almost through the door, the way a groom would. As if coming into his house was really something after I refused for so long. It made me happy.

I don't often get an invitation to go somewhere. And to a séance! What to wear? I have to say looking ridiculous has its pluses too. People don't want to look at me, and I make them. It's a power.

36

Aphra arrives at our door in her moth costume, toned down for street wear, feelers removed, the snaps that turn the sleeves into wings unsnapped, but still a costume—it's a séance after all, an occasion for costumes. She couldn't resist the invitation to hear from my brother—or to see us fail to conjure him. He'll never talk to you, she says. You're all so gullible.

My son doesn't hear this. He is slumped to one side at the séance table and under headphones, attached to his screen until the very last minute. He has to attend, because he is the direct link to his uncle, at least in her eyes. I'm trapped, he says with his own. But he came around to helping with my plan and hopes it will work—we hope it will turn Aphra away for good.

The living dead? says Aphra, who points at one of his on-screen zombies. I can show you some moves.

He grunts, about as noncommittal a sound a human can make.

Her smile crosses the whole of her broad face. I see now he's really why she agreed to the craziness of a séance so easily, him and the opportunity to return to our house and call us gullible. Okay, if that's what it takes. But we're not going to be able to hold the séance at all if I can't get my mother to turn down the TV in the next room. So religious when it comes to the occult and thus anti-, my mother has declared herself appalled and concedes to lower the volume only after I break the seal on a new bottle.

Her wrist is too sore from opening so many.

After that quick hiatus, I say Okay to the assembled. This includes a medium I have already paid who wears a turban and has set up a big clear ball on top of a shawl spread in the middle of the dining room table where a turkey might go. I turn down the lights, and my son removes his headphones.

This medium intones her instructions: we touch fingertips, we bow our heads, we try not to giggle. The first sign that there's a problem is that Aphra won't sway when the medium begins to and tells everyone to follow. Aphra sits cold, as if the energy emanating from the ball solders her in place. Her fingers stop touching mine and start drumming.

But she's listening.

My son has taken a tape from long ago and edited it with two boom boxes, taking and rearranging my brother's words, fashioning a ransom-letter project in sound until it says what we want. My son helped with the voice too—it is enough like his uncle's when it goes low. However, somehow in making these tapes, he gets the background of a dog howling. To my son, this howling is just a technical difficulty. It scares only me, the burning of the Shove-It boys and the wild dog still running at the edge of my windshield, literal and figurative.

I make what could be seen by Aphra and my son as a shiver.

The medium puts out her first question: Are you tormented?

A distant argument from my mother's TV answers.

What? says the medium anyway, and she cocks her head. You should find someone older? He's what? The medium goes on in this vein, with her *whats* all roundabout references to my son and his suffering, nodding in between, affirming her stance as a listener with a far off gaze.

My son avoids looking at anyone. Not that he would want to.

Finally, a disembodied voice comes out of the ball and announces what we know is recorded: You should be ashamed, the last word sounding as if it were made from *ass* and *maimed* but more likely *ask* and *named*.

Aphra's hands go flat to the table as if to hold it down, but then, instead of a bowed head or a blush, she pushes away from the table and stands. He always said that to me, she says.

How do I know what my brother said?

Shame is something you own is what you told me, she says, addressing my brother directly. You have it, and you should be proud of it, because it is yours. You said that all the time.

Concentrate, commands the medium, clutching at her ball with chipped nails.

Aphra eases herself back down.

Is there something anyone else would like to say to their dearly beloved? asks the medium.

I ask whether he's happy where he is, and there's silence. My son asks whether it was okay for us to have sold his hot tub, and there's more silence.

I'm sorry I kissed you, says Aphra.

There's the sound of a big juicy buss. Everyone but Aphra goes stock-still. He's here, says Aphra.

My son opens his eyes wide. TV? he mouths to me.

I ignore him.

The medium is not happy. She scratches where her turban presses her forehead, and the recorded voice takes over again. *I have seen you look at my nephew*, says the voice. *Ass-maimed*, it says again.

He looks just like you. I can't help it. Aphra is matter-of-fact. I just want to—

Uh-huh, interrupts the medium. She goes off script and croons that she believes in being more open about your wants. Be open, she says to Aphra. Open yourself to love and your soul to shame, she says, if that's what he's telling you. Open up to it. What do you want? Be open, says the medium.

Aphra whips open those big arms of hers and says, What I want—

One arm slams into the woman's tilted Sears turban in such a way that the turban tumbles off, showing the woman's forehead embossed by the press of the jewel and a crown of pink curlers. Worse, the recorder flops out from under the turban where it plays *ask-named, ask-named* on the floor. We all stare at the downed machine for as long as it takes to hear the repeat twice, and then it gives a doggy howl and quits. In our return silence, the medium says, Call me if you need anything else, rolls what is most likely just a plastic crystal ball back into its bowling bag, and leaves.

Well, that was fun, says Aphra in the middle of that. She dusts off her costume, flips her hair off her neck, one lank lock after another, and makes for the door, which she slams.

My son blank-eyes me. That wasn't getting it out in the open—that was making us ask-named, he says.

I'm sorry, I say. It was a bad idea. But where did that extra sound, that kiss, come from?

I don't know, says my son. I don't care. Him?

My mother teeters in just then, clinking her ice with authority. My second cousin sat on a jury that put away a woman like that who wouldn't stop calling her ex. But, says my mother, it's hard to get men to show any interest at all these days. She shoves the glass my way. For example, men do not call you.

Mom's old, says my son, collecting his computer and his earphones.

Thanks, I say with a sigh.

She's divorced. My mother spits out the word as if I have a big D in red on my chest, one that also means Dumb. And Disgusting. And Degraded.

I catch her glass before she drops it. Mom!

That big woman who was here doesn't have the future on her side, she says, teetering, and your brother knew it. She retrieves her glass with a thank you meant only for help. He is lucky he's dead.

My son leaves the room and shuts his bedroom window loudly so the whole house can hear it, as if Aphra would climb through and hide under his bed. Then he exits the house for the car of a friend who must have been idling nearby since he appears so quickly. The car's music booms so he can't possibly hear what might sound like unhappiness coming from me, who is very sorry such a crazy idea was just crazy.

37

Mom locks me out. She stands on the porch with the key, her new key.

I start to cry. I know what's left for me as work, and it's not as if Mom will say no to that either. Being too old for that now, she takes in ironing, but hardly anyone needs that done anymore, except the clergy. She charges double for them, because it's always embroidered.

Your boyfriend's moving in? Really?

She doesn't look at me like she's shit-proud, the way she should. She doesn't answer right away; then she does. Dad is getting out of jail, and you put him there. And where else is he going to go?

Him? I say. He's coming back?

He wasn't so bad.

What about me?

What about me? says Mom.

When I don't say anything back, she says, You were a flirt. When I still don't say anything, she says just as loud, Get out of here. You're almost forty, too old to live with me.

Oh, for the good old days of social services.

After I stuff everything of mine from the closet floor into a bag, along with my toothbrush in the bathroom, and put it into the back seat of Sport, she throws my butterfly costume out the window, still on the hanger, as if that's what I really need.

Now I sit in Sport.

When I finish crying, I think to myself, Good idea. I will move to a bigger town, maybe even two hundred miles away, where I can be big, as big as I want. And safe.

But then I think, Not right away. I still have a little money from her brother that he gave me for driving him around—bless him to bits.

I never told my mother that, or she would have taken it for rent. Or for back rent, all the way back to when I was born.

I can always use the bathrooms I clean in the motel for a shower, but I have to wait until they call me in. You can wash quite a bit of yourself at the filling station—nobody stops you. Soap is cheap from the canister, except when it is the ground-up kind and hard to wash off. A lot of food comes in packages you can microwave at the filling station but quick so they don't see you're not buying their big-money burritos. I like carrots. They're good for the eyes, and that's what I've got going the best, sitting in my car. I have my phone too, and the plan doesn't run out for weeks. In SACK *the leader showed everybody how to list whatever we came up with to do on the phone, any old thing, and put it in a plan—one, two, three.*

What can I do? I make a list.

38

In our tiny school, we shared a classroom every other year—first–second grade, third–fourth grade, fifth–sixth grade, seventh–eighth grade—and it must have been in the fifth or sixth grade when we read a story in the *Weekly Reader* about a boy stuck at the bottom of a mine and of how he was a hero for eating whatever could be lowered to him, and for waiting for somebody to figure out how to get him out without squashing him. Except, of course, as our teacher pointed out, he should not have fallen into the mine in the first place. It was his own fault that he fell in. He didn't just stroll by and end up down a mine shaft, did he? But he was a hero to us for a while, despite whatever he did to get there, and then because the *Weekly Reader* was religious, the next one asked us to pray for his dear departed soul.

My brother was that boy: those birds in their cages so close, needing air, the shaft so deep, so far away equal to a guy unloading radioactive materials, an electric-charged brain, and then life with Aphra. Like the boy in the shaft, no last rites were involved in his dying, a good Catholic reason to want to come up for more air.

When we stopped praying for that boy in the hole, we started praying to the boy in the hole.

It was the gray and nothing way my brother saw things that made him want to dig instead of getting any other job. It was the only thing he could do that no one would ask him how well he did it, and he could still be a nothing and be paid for it. *Not a thing at all.* As long as he didn't fall into his hole, as deep as it was, getting deeper. As long as he could make fill and not take it.

It must have been dark at the bottom of that hole. He was at the bottom of the hole for a long time in that dark, digging, fearing that bird going dead in its cage.

What? is all I can say now. Maybe I'm just being selfish, but I want his part of my history explained. Will what happened to you happen to me? If I knew exactly what it was, I could prepare myself and fend it off.

Let's not talk about it, says my father every time.

But we have to talk—Aphra is after us.

I am driving ten miles away to shop at a new grocery store. My father drives to work a half hour early to deliver my son to school, my son pressing himself flat to the floor of the car. Even my mother plays hard of hearing when Aphra insists on trailing behind her to the liquor store, for Aphra is now dogging all of us. What does she want from us now?

My son begs us to never talk to her again. My father says he will get Aphra's license revoked, and my mother will break Aphra's legs with her wax cane, which she threatens to make as soon as her wax supplies arrive. But really, they're all too busy to be bothered.

A restraining order, I decide, is just the ticket.

The judge understands. Things must have changed since my brother tried to get such an order. Or else she is less attractive to law enforcement.

three

39

Yes, Officer.

He doesn't like me sitting under the railroad turnaround. He says I need to go home. I am not causing any trouble, am I? I ask so politely.

He doesn't answer.

I move Sport out to a country road, to give the cop a rest, while I rest. It's the same guy who wanted to know about the exploded car and the boys. He wasn't so bad. At least he didn't say I did anything.

No lights anywhere out here. It's like I'm the only one in the whole wide world. My court order says I have to stay fifty feet away from his family, but I'm fifty feet from everybody everywhere. That seems like nothing in the dark open space of all these stars. It still makes me lonely, and I miss people, even Mom, even though she likes Dad better than me—that's plain as day. I think about Dad moving around in my bedroom, touching things, looking at my posters. When he wanted me, that was something. Otherwise, he put me out of his head. If jail helps a man like that, I don't know how. Back then, Mom was all—I don't know. He didn't do it most of the time.

The next a.m., I ask the Spanish lady I work with if she's seen a shovel anywhere around the motel. I use sign language and pretend digging, because I don't know the Spanish words. She isn't exactly helpful. She has a cousin or a friend she wants to get hired instead of me, so why would she be? But she keeps her baby in her car while she works, and she's always going out there to check on him. That at least gives me a chance to sneak into the shower. I get that done, and then I have a little look-see in the equipment closet on my own. All there is, is a snow shovel.

I guess I can't be too picky.

40

At the Holiday Inn two ladies from the capitol are talking about all the art we could display or have performed in this town if we could just get ourselves organized right so that the state could pour money into what seems to be a car that runs on art. They have charts to show how the engine works and the destinations, like symphonies. It's not the kind of talk you would expect half the audience to turn off their screens for, but there they all are, their dirty secret bare: a lust for art, yes, and it could be theirs if the state pours real money into what seems to be a pretty good car when you think about it.

I collect one of the already-poured plastic-cupped wines in the back and sip it in a seat at the front, where I'd be least likely open to an Aphra attack. Two weeks ago the cops served the restraining order, but they told us she was so polite and happy to see them, it was as if she had been delivered pizza. She sets out each morning to find us, with a measuring tape she waves that must be fifty feet long, to show she is not breaking the order.

Yes, she has been raped. I drop any euphemism—she shouted it to me over our fifty feet. Of course she's angry at everyone—no one protected her or offered her sympathy, no girl, woman, or child, no man or husband or mother. Just my brother. Or did she make that up too, the same kind of story like the one about how she found a nail clipping in the toothpaste, or the dog that licked a hole in her skirt? The police did grin, I was told, when they made their report. I tend to believe all the stories that passed from high schooler to high schooler when I was that age, because we didn't have the imagination we have now from the internet. If so, she raised herself up from being the victim to the far side of bully—to monster. Still, her lover has died, probably her only ever. She is harassing us because she has to—she wants us to take the place of him. It's all very rational, as long as I'm not facing her.

I'm going to get a life. In art.

Where better to start than art in situ, where ladies of my ilk in humanities might be friendly, and even men. A few of them have probably heard about the séance, not to mention the burned boys' earlier accusations. The Halloween party with its theft of donations has turned legend. However, the now uncostumed man from that party is in attendance, although his witch is, too, drink in hand, and in the break, she has turned to talk to someone else. I sidle near him and start talking about how hard it is to transfer art from the big cities, how what looks like experiment there tends to look really untenable here, and he's smiling. But then the witch pivots and leans forward in a way that says she knows that he screwed on my head at that party, and she shakes my hand and says how sorry she is to have to cut the whole art thing short. She has an office to go to tomorrow.

She leaves, but he doesn't.

I am standing on an ice floe, surrounded on all sides by the water of feeling instead of land. Great, I say to him, or something equally dumb.

Take your seats, please.

The ladies from the capitol clear their throats and go on to part 2 to finish explaining their art car, and then they ask for questions. I am reckless with the man showing up, our own almost talk, and a sense of competition with the witch, and there is also the wine. I ask, Is this the kind of art that you have to enjoy or the kind that unsettles you, making you turn your head differently at every rose and tree? Does the state come and impound that car if what it does unsettles everyone? Or is this car another something made out of nothing, paint and scrap wood and two kinds of glass, a car after a crash that someone gets up to sell, saying this is something and not junk? Of course I couch this talk so they all get it.

I listen to their answers, nodding, using my brother's gray-grit part of me, a way of looking that two children share even when they're not sharing, when one set of eyes are gone and the other's are going. Listening to these ladies from the capitol answer me with the benefits of this art car, how it swallows whole all the pluses and minuses of everyday living and makes the days good enough to enjoy, makes me think that art is where my brother should have disappeared into, where he could have lived. After all, it was where my mother wanted to live, but we came along and made her a nothing.

I take another sip, and glance at the guy a row up. What a nice neck of his own.

Someone else asks what this art will cost, and the ladies pull out the projections that dead-end every presentation. Then we all stand up and mill again. I smile and down my second drink. I am headed for the wedge of space around the refills that has opened up around the man, but as I elbow up awkwardly, someone explains, by way of *whatever*, that his sister has left.

Oh.

I am thinking I'll give him the sly-eye, but before I can blind myself to possible rejection, he nods goodbye, too, and wades out of the crowd. Discarding my plastic cup like *opportunity wasted* or *in pursuit*, I head for the door after him. What am I going to say? Two steps away from him, Aphra thrusts another drink at me. That is, she sashays right through the placarded party room, and all the town ladies, chatting in their town best—and me, near the exit, wearing what I would call an art-potential dress in a single color—almost stop talking. Aphra is holding that restraining order next to the drink glass as if it is my check, offering it over a stack of folded chairs much closer than the fifty feet she is supposed to come.

I want to dig him up, she whispers before I can flee or play dead or call the cops. That's all I wanted to ask you, she says in another desperate sotto voce whisper.

What are you doing here?

I work here, she says.

Right. I take the drink from her hand before it slips from her grip. This what she wants, this is why she has been harassing us all these weeks? You could have written a letter, I say to her through my clenched teeth, as the ladies restart their chat, as if she would have. Sent me an email. Put a note on the door.

She plants her hands on her hips. She is not smiling.

I am not really surprised at her request. After all, this kind of digging is the town's wont—it's a town built on digging, let alone hers, let alone his. But digging up? They've always dug down and in. That's illegal, I say. I think.

She throws up a hand as if the law is a mere inconvenience. Since he spoke to me at the séance, she says, I decided. I used to think if I could just look at the sky and see him, I would be all right. I think he's not underground, but I have to find out, which means I have to dig him up to check. That's all I have to do. Then I'll be happy.

I think you have to get a court order to dig him up.

She says maybe that's true, but—

I take a sip.

Is there a latch on the coffin? she asks. The dirt is probably still pretty loose. It hasn't snowed yet.

I take two more sips. The drink's much stronger than the first two, but now, instead of drinking away the irrational fear of talking to these local ladies who are so interested in art, or the fear I have of the man with the neck not finding me attractive, the fear goes more personal. It's Aphra's irrational self I have to deal with, but also my own *Why did he die?* that teeters around her question. I don't have my mother's problem with drinking—I have the problem of drinking too few drinks that make quick decisions difficult.

Aphra doesn't move. I take yet another sip. Digging him up might make her see that it's him down there, his face and not my son's, and that my brother's really dead. Whatever step was left out in her grieving could be put back in with the dirt this time, stamped down for good. On the really big plus side, if she digs him up, maybe she'll go to jail and leave us alone.

I could ask for an autopsy.

You have to come, she says. She tells me all about this idea of hers—that if I'm there while she does it, then it's not an attempt to defile the body, it's fine, it's a relative, it's okay.

Whoa. I shake my head hard against that one. That's baloney.

She makes what in polite society would be called a hiss.

I start thinking about seeing Aphra again tomorrow morning, waiting fifty feet from our doorstep, about going to the store and seeing her waiting beside the produce. Restraining order or not, in a small town, you can't hide from this kind of will. If you promise not to harass us any more, I say, maybe sometime—

Tonight, she says, and she grabs my forearm so hard I can feel a bruise start and my drink splashes the art car that is just about to drive off as these two ladies are towing it past me, packing up with their placards—splashes in a rather nice pattern that the ladies lunge forward to daub off the laminate.

All the other ladies back away.

Excuse me, says Aphra. I left my lights on. She takes my forearm again and plunges me and herself past the others at the door. My lights, she says so everyone understands why the drink was spilled and sort of why we are both barging out of the reception. By the time we get to the lobby, even I am convinced of car malfeasance—I offer her a jump start.

Ha, she says, and out the door we traipse to the parking lot. She opens the passenger side of her car and slams me into it, before her *Ha!* hits me it's mocking. Whatever. She drives away humming, with me a little dizzy and bearing confused dread.

The car smells.

Wait, I say when we pull past my car.

She lets me out, and instead of fleeing, I get the shovel out of the back. His, I'm thinking, from the time when the dog was on fire. I don't know what she's bringing, but this is one tool we'll definitely need.

In five minutes, we're at the gates where he's buried, and then through the gates. She parks beside the plot that abuts the abandoned drive-in, and kills the motor. Its tick, tick afterward says *silence*. There's a new moon.

41

Has Aphra put something she bought from the Shove-Its into my sips of wine? A sort of date-rape pill that makes everything you set out to do seem okay? I look out over my cup at the drive-in beside the cemetery in her rearview mirror, its weedy saplings sprouting up as tall as the audio posts between the slight tilt of the car stalls. In wafts, I get the memory of the drive-in before it closed, when the parked and tilted station wagons always looked ready for burial—we used to say so, leaning back with our boyfriends.

That was before my brother took up digging.

To be buried in your place of work—that's an ambition I didn't know my brother had but the kind of ambition someone who thought he was nothing might have.

At least nobody's here, Aphra says after she rolls down her window.

Of course the dead drive-in gives off no noise—there's not a ping of sound after the car shivers off. Aphra gets out and rummages through the trunk while I decide the huge screen-back looks like something ancient—Cleopatran, a leaning monument, with thin boards and beams across the back that barely hold it up, blank, a celebration of the long dead, a tombstone itself. Then I'm thinking about all the settlers, so settled.

There's Aphra, tapping at my window.

I would look over my shoulder but not here. That's for people in the movies—that's for people doing something bad. I don't want to be part of this, I say after I roll the window down. It's such a bad idea.

Trim digging is what he did, Aphra says. She's cradling a snow shovel in the crook of her arm. He smoothed the dirt under the sod, she says, and made the edges crisp. Most of the dirt digging was done with the backhoe and just needed light hand shoveling, but the winters weren't easy, she says. Like rolling the rock back, he used to tell me, only with no roll in that rock.

I nod. I say, Good, as if I mean it. Snow shovel?

In the summer, I used to come and watch him work, she says. Why, over here, she says, shifting her weight to the right and pointing with her snow shovel, he shoveled out the whole hole, a custom job.

Go on, I say. I drink the rest of the drink.

Doc Lewart wanted a round hole. He wanted his time capsules to go down with him, one attached to either side. And they didn't use a machine on the petrified people either, she says, leaning into the window, her whole face now in my face again. Your brother dug them up by hand.

The petrified people were from before he started, I say, the wine making me smile. They were dug up when we were in high school. They were pioneers, I think, who turned into rock.

It was during high school, yes, she says. You were probably a senior then and too busy with your own stuff. What happened was he answered an ad. He shoveled out the two big truckloads of dirt where they couldn't use the machine, she says. It was in the paper. He did it so good they had to hire him after.

I pop the door just to get her to move. I guess I didn't know that, I say. I never knew why he went into digging. I decide to get out, to move around. It's chilly, and the wind cuts the wine buzz. What's Aphra saying?

She is speaking into the night, but then she turns. Front page when he found the second one. You saw her—a woman you couldn't get a shovel into if you took a jackhammer to her. They proved that at the fair that very year.

I am standing outside the car in the near freezing but far enough away that my white breath doesn't touch hers. It was in a tent, I nod. You had to pay to have a look. I forgot he had all that attention.

I didn't pay, she said.

I nod like *of course*. Didn't he dodge her? Didn't he dodge her all high school? I give the stars a stare. Maybe he was looking for more petrified people all the rest of the time he was digging, I say. Like a kind of archaeologist.

She's hulking, her huge shadow solid beside me. No, she says, close enough I can see her face, the certainty of the no.

I see Doc Lewart's normal-looking stone not so far off.

Aphra's peering into the hatchback of her car. He used to use your kind of shovel. She points inside.

I found it, I say. Near the meteor hole.

She takes it out of the back and walks with it, along with her snow shovel, over to the grave site. Pretty hard to find, so really, she's spent some time here.

I avoid looking at the graves nearby. They make me dizzy. I concentrate on the dead cornstalks across the road from the entrance of the graveyard, their long ragged shadows in the moonlight, the moon itself. I'm elsewhere, some moon-laden place conjured up by those sips of wine, but I follow her anyway. I don't want to be left alone in the moon-dark, getting sober.

She's already tossed down both shovels and picked up hers. And I don't know how, but she shoves it into the sod. How could a snow shovel dig? She pulls back on the handle as if that's all there is to it, but of course, the sod doesn't yield to that kind of shovel the way the sod looks like it should. She tries shoving in what there is of a point, one of the corners—she shoves it in harder. It glances off.

I try not to watch, but I take my eyes off the moon in wonder.

She shovels yet again and unearths just a few clods. It's harder than I thought, she says. I never tried to do what he did. She sniffles. She's not so cheerful when she struggles. She makes a tiny sob I almost don't hear. I don't know, she says. I didn't think you'd let me. She throws down the shovel.

We'll both get arrested, as if that's any consolation. I pat her. I pat and pat all over her vast back until she blows her nose.

People are always trying to dig up Jim Morrison's grave, she says.

We shouldn't be here, Aphra. I have to go to work tomorrow. Aren't you working these days?

She says, Today is Tuesday. I do beds mostly on the odd days.

A dog is howling somewhere.

These days the nights are all alike, I say. With what I have to do in the world, with you following us nonstop.

You could dig too, she says. Maybe it runs in the family.

Ha, I laugh, with plenty of disbelief. I have the regular hands of a lady, which is to say they are not digging hands—but in my present woozy condition and with Aphra sniffling beside me, I can't resist a try, if only to show her how easy it is. I use the shovel I found. It turns out I have to jump on where the blade's attached, to make it dig deep enough into the sod to turn it. Once you get past the sod, the dirt is still fluffy from all those months ago when he was buried. It's not so hard digging with this shovel. Because it's his?

If I dig him up, I think, maybe he can be tested for some powerful aphrodisiac. That must have been the problem: her.

No roll in that rock, she says, the way she says he used to say it. I'll get the plastic from the car to keep the dirt together.

She's thought this far ahead. I am not thinking much at all—those drinks are doing the thinking.

I jig the shovel into a sand pocket. My brother did this for a living? He wasn't digging graves, I decide. He was digging for valuables, the way he dug up the Chinese firecracker—like digging for gold, for a petrified person. Digging for himself. Or for someone to love? He had me, albeit not around. He had his father and sometimes his mother. Love, so to speak. He even had a nephew who looked like him. But if I needed more—and I did, quite a bit more—why wouldn't he?

Where is Aphra?

I dig some more. Rocks deciding what rock to be turn darker in the layers of dirt I uncover. I find old wrappers. Happy-enough worms. Aphra's peach pit? I hold it in front of me and try to think of something important to say about death or even life, a soliloquy. After all, it's a peach pit. But I can't come up with anything to quote, other than *To be or not*, so I toss it away.

She spreads the plastic right down to the edge and sits beside it. It looks as if we're involved in some kind of night picnic, until I start shoveling the dirt onto the tarp. She moves a little farther away. Brushing her hair off her face with a dirty hand back, she tells me about how she would lie down next to his hole while he shoveled, how he said he could control radio signals by swinging the shovel just so, how the stars would blink after a while from his swinging, and soon she would think she was in one of those trains that roar past the town—blink, blink, blink—instead of under stars, the train going so fast that he would have to come and save her.

My birthday is just eleven months before his, I say, shoveling.

Not much turnaround. She bends to toss back a clod that has humped up at her feet.

I just dug that out.

It was romantic, she says. The way he was.

She tells me that he told her I sometimes sleepwalked with my eyes open and my arms out like this—she holds her hands out like a zombie. And once he found me like that at the top of the stairs about to jump, and he held me back.

I don't think the bit by the stairs was a rescue, I say. I think he was giving me a choice, to do what he wanted or to get a push.

Aphra frowns as if she doesn't believe me.

It comes to me that he had a game he called guillotine, I say, where we would put our fingers under the window and try to pull them away before he closed it. That's the kind of game he liked, I say. Of course, he was different with you.

She nods. She says that by me telling her things about him, it keeps him alive for her. My not having much good to tell about him shows how little I knew my brother—the bad things stand out like a bang on a nail of a finger from a window that makes a mark that never goes away until one day it's clipped off, that brown or black part. What was the good part again?

He took out my trash for me, she says. He knew the names of all the stray dogs after his cat ran off. He looked at my chewed nails and said, Nervous? Once another girl liked him—I just knew it. She put tin can curlings in his soup at the café he was always eating lunch in with your dad.

No way, I say. Those were in my soup too. Those girls were married.

Okay, she says without much agreement. So what color were his eyes?

Gray, I say. Red-rimmed from allergies.

Ha, she says. Ha, ha. So brown.

More of the little I know or ever knew gets dug up.

42

I dig more while I can, before her laughing starts to bother me, before I think too much about this woman and the dark and this hole, before I get too sober. He read the encyclopedia to go to sleep at night, I say, but he never got past G. By the time you get to G, he would say, you knew everything—all the other words have already been talked about. That's how it was with him—if you knew one thing, you knew all the others.

I dig two more shovelfuls, and she's silent.

She's not talking about his spells, the ones he had to have had with her, the terror of them, the predead twitching and the talking, the tongue you had to catch. She's not talking about his trip to the Gulf or his electrocution.

No other girl would have him, she says, as if she knows my thoughts.

I'm covered with his dirt the way the whole town must be—at least the dirt he dug—every time it blows. But some of it's his especially. The more I dig, the more that dirt might be his, or at least next to his. All this dirt everywhere keeps me from seeing how much I didn't love him alive, how I shunned him, as if this face I wear now shows it in blankness. No one can say I'm not friendly, says the face.

No one can say I am.

Aphra could be a friend. My brother could have been saying *care*, as in *care for her. Dare you to*, maybe he didn't say. All this time, wondering who he was, I have to dig him up to find out.

The hole yawns, as they say, but with indifference, as if I could be next, as if I am next. This is pretty far down, I say. How far down is he?

You can't see out. That's the rule. She's now standing beside the hole, which is pitiful, which isn't really deep at all.

You made that up. That's movie talk. I unzip my jacket. At least I'm not cold anymore.

You know, you don't look like him, she says. Not a bit. You could even not be related.

Except for my son, I say. And how he looks.

She wallops the edge of the plastic sheet to settle the dirt in the middle.

The digging I'm doing doesn't lay around what I know, in little chunks or time capsules. Instead, what I know gets spread out and confused in the broadcast of all this dirt. By digging, I decide, by my being him in the digging, I steal even that nothing from him. I make even that mine.

I'm finished, I say. I look at the jagged pit, because that's what a hole is, even after all this time. Do you think they'll arrest us?

Lots of people will want to arrest us. You want to arrest me.

She throws her feet over the side and falls forward and in, right beside me, and she begins to dig again herself, this time with a dog approach, the shovel as a scoop between her legs. Dirt sprays out, wide and high.

I could flee. Instead, I stand to one side in the pit, curious, too curious. How can such a small hole produce so much dirt? There's dirt all over the place—we'll never get all this dirt back into the hole and cover our tracks. But Aphra has spread her plastic well. She has a plan with that plastic. She is good with plans. I hope.

She rests against the wall of the hole. I have to lever her out—I actually help her with a shove to her bottom. Then, getting purchase on the edge with her elbows, she heaves herself over and pants, Dear God.

She gives me the chance to be the final digger, to locate him myself.

I'll find him. If I can figure out how he died, I'll be free. If I know who to blame, I'll stop blaming myself. But maybe it is my fault: I killed him by shunning him. So what if brothers die all the time, shunned or unshunned. This one's mine. I'm dizzy with argument, not drink. I am on the scene and so close to discovery. If I can confront Aphra with its wreckage, then I'll be able to tell what really happened at the end by watching her.

I go back in with my blisters and my by-now stiff back, and I shovel more, and fiercely.

If I complained about my brother's fighting, my mother would say all boys fight.

Served him right, I thought, whenever he had a spell.

Then I moved away and married someone who beat me. I didn't tell my father about that little detail, just the way I didn't complain to my father about my brother beating me. I married my brother. Oh, brother—to be free of you. I raise the shovel for one more go. I shovel and shovel, and I hit metal.

Its *ting* scares me. I drop the shovel and back away, but not far. You can't back away very far in such a hole.

Is that him? asks Aphra, her face now a white wedge above the dark dirt rim. He could be petrified himself by now, she says, sniffing. There's a lot of calcium down there, all that white stuff.

No way, I say. I'm too tired to talk about how long that takes with calcium, how the petrified ones weren't buried in his kind of box. I look up at Aphra's face. You sure you want to do this? I ask. Open the coffin?

I have to kiss him, she says, but then she backs away from the edge until I can't see her. I hear her vomit. She's thinking with her stomach—she's deciding.

The shovel keeps on shoveling—I can't help but lift it again. I have to shovel more now that he's so close, if just to show her, to call her bluff. Kissing? I think. That's radical.

There's the sound of hit metal again, but this time a lot of water gushes into the bottom of the hole. I shovel at it, because wet soil shovels easier—it just doesn't shovel out so well, being so heavy. Then water covers the bottom.

Aphra peers over the side. Get out! It's the Captain Kidd problem—the hole is cursed so that every time anybody digs into it, water fills it up.

The wet sucks at my shoes, and I tell her it's probably me hitting the underground sprinklers. They are buried deep because of frost. What do you think? Tape up the pipe if I find it? I ask her, over the gushing. I might be able to fix it and keep going.

She disappears again from the edge. She leaves me.

I lean against the wall of the hole, rest against the side. I'm not thinking about my ankles and how my brother's hands could come up out of the coffin, and take me down to as deep as he is. I look up. The moon has the clouds fighting each other, vapor on vapor. If I can see them fight, I'll stay calm, if still a little dizzy—I won't think about my brother's hands so much.

Aphra, I call out. Aphra.

I kick footholds into the sides, making a kind of stairs with the chinks. When I finally rise on my filthy palms out of the pit of my own making, I see Aphra sitting by the car unbraiding the nylon webbing that holds together the grave lawn mower she's dragged over. The webbing shreds as she unties it—it's so plastic and wild she has to braid it back up at the same time.

I was going to pull you out with this rope. She sticks the stub of nylon toward where I'm standing, shivering. But now we can go.

I thought you had to kiss him.

She drops her made-up rope, and it instantly unbraids. She picks it up again, starts over. She doesn't look at me, shivering and filthy and panting. He's full of preservatives, isn't he?

He was full of preservatives at the service, I say, trying to wipe my hands clean on the grass. You should've kissed him then.

Maybe when we open it, his cheeks will still be pink, a miracle like a saint's, she says. She's watching her hands braiding the nylon, so serious, as if she braids for a living.

I say, He probably won't look as good as he did when they laid him out.

Aphra stares over my shoulder at the site.

I brush my hands together, most of the dirt sticking.

You still have to dig out around it, she says to me, so we have room to get the lid open.

When I do nothing, she shifts her body toward me and the site, the braided rope wriggling in her hand like a pigtail. I suppose all the water will get in if we open it.

Right, I say. You'd have to lift it out.

Aphra nods her head back toward me, and her big tears well in the moonlight that runs over her.

43

It is the burned Shove-It boys, the Hoods, who catch us. There is no reason why they're out so late or here, other than it's a Tuesday night and you can drive fast on the stretch beside the cemetery, you can strip gears, or you can park on the dark side and do whatever you want without anyone interrupting. They don't tip tombstones—that would be too obvious trouble-of-their-own-making.

No taillights appear on their car until they stomp on the brake, having slid in front of us on the long winding road that Aphra takes out, all the dirt packed back into the site and the sod carefully smashed together on top, the two of us now in a big hurry to go. Both sets of wheels screech and stop. One of the boys gets out, wearing his hood, and examines the half inch left between our bumpers. I get out, too, and say what a big hearse they have there.

The cold's so sharp at my senses I can smell the weed he's been smoking three feet away. He takes his eyes off the near miss and puts them on the caked stuff falling off my front, my soaked-through shoes, and he whistles. Instead of saying, *I know what you've been up to*, he says, Are you loaded?

This must be a drug term, because of course I don't appear to have much in the way of money, with total exhaustion replacing being drunk as my look. But unfolded from the hearse, he is large enough to make his point, or any point, unreasonably tall, like all boys my son's age.

He knows what we need—a clean exit.

Are you deaf? he asks with his hand to his ear on one side, as if he is. Your money? he says, and a second kid gets out of the car, just as hulking.

Hey, he says.

Just then, Aphra hauls herself out too, but her size, her usual strategy in a one-on-one, does not work so well in the dark, with these two.

Oh, you, says the second boy, with the disgust I remember boys had for her when I was his age. He puts a hand up as if to keep her away, a hand with strange webbing, little hammocks of skin that doctors make after burns.

She steps back into the cornstalks.

Don't they use corn in drugs? I ask out of the blue to distract them, to make me seem interested in their probable pastime.

The second kid says I'm right—there are drugs made from corn, along with corn oil and popcorn. He learned about it in class last week. He says this as if he is sure we are under our own corn influence. The police scanner in the hearse squawks. Now, are we going to have to drive over there—he points toward where the flashing lights of a cop car might have just disappeared—and say something to my dad about what you've been up to?

I pull a few wadded bills out of my back pocket, as well as receipts, that the first kid plucks out from my hand like lint, and he hands the money to the second.

Hey, says the second kid again, and he jerks his head toward Aphra, who has been stock-still ever since she figured out who they were.

She finds and unties a bag from around her neck and between her breasts. I was saving this to buy from you.

Ha, says the second kid. Ha, ha.

So they are the ones, their fake laugh admits.

The knots take her so long I have time to look at the two burned boys at length. The hoods make the burns scarier, a kind of this-could-be-worse glimpse of wads of skin. The kid's webby hands drop coins while he tries to count them.

Forget that, the first boy says, taking Aphra's pouch away from him, emptying it into his own hand, and throwing the pouch into the ditch. He then pushes her away to paw through her car's insides for whatever he can find.

The moon rises while we wait, the three of us watching the hind end of the boy wriggle as he works.

I don't have any drugs, Aphra says.

I nod.

They won't even sell them to me most of the time, she says.

Bitch, says the first burned boy, exiting the car. Bitch, bitch, bitch, he says to us, coming up close, very close. He steps right up to Aphra's face.

Maybe it is the *bitch* that changes her.

She has something hidden in her fist, and she flicks it on, right next to his nose. I should have left you in that fire, she says. She shoves the lighter close.

Fuck, he says. He throws his hands over his face, he staggers into me. Fuck you, too, he says, turning on me. But Aphra moves the lighter with him, thrusting it hard at his hair. He flails at her, at the lighter. Backing into the hearse, he gets his hood caught in the door, has to open and shut it twice getting in, and the second kid, furious, the smell of his friend's singed hair everywhere, retreats too. I'm telling my dad, the second boy screeches from the passenger's seat. Then Aphra comes up and flicks the lighter very close to his window.

I collect the lost coins in their exhaust.

Let me, she says, and she picks up the rest of the money with energy I just don't have, shaking with fear and the cold and relief. She hands the coins to me so sweetly that it is as if this moment of cornstalks-gone-dark and the rising hearse exhaust and the dirt in our clothes mixed with the sweat of fear and the sweat of hard work will run us together forever.

Thank you, I say.

She flicks her lighter on again, and I see a woman who is tired and no longer young—like me. Then the last of the light gives me a glimpse of how dirty we both are, how clearly it shows we've been digging. Together.

Leave my boy alone, I say.

Standing there, I watch Aphra think about what I said with her face, and it is not what I want to see.

44

Some day in the future—way, way forward—Earth people will X-ray the ground and find all these boxes of bones. Why did we put the people we loved away so deep? Why not have the box in the living room or bedroom, where you can at least talk to what's inside? Or keep it at the mall for a while, so a lot of people could get used to whoever being dead? I guess "it" is the problem—you don't get to talk to the person inside anymore. It's that silence you put in the ground that you have to get used to.

Thinking sci-fi like that always calms me down. My feelings lose air like one of those fancy egg white dishes that collapse if you open the oven door. You open the oven of the present by thinking of something past or future. Why, I could be a pioneer lady in a bonnet from a long time ago and have to leave him behind on the trail, never to be found again, until he's petrified.

I start to cry, and have to curl the tip of my shirt up to wipe my face. Sport and me are parked across the street from my house, where my dad is living now. He just came out and waved at me like Go away. *Dressed in those tan pants men just out of jail wear and a white shirt and loafers, he looks ready for interviews, probably the same ones I'm trying for. I stop a sob. I want my mom to come out and say she's sorry she kicked me out, because of course she is or soon will be. Dad is still angry for sure and will soon hit her, because that's what he does. But she's getting what she wants, so I can't feel sorry for her. I decide to check the mailbox, which she hardly ever checks, because why should she except for pulling out bills she can't pay? It would drive her crazy to see me pretending to still live here.*

At the very back, I find a letter with my name on it. It is torn and dirty and wet after the rainstorm we had a week ago that leaked into the mailbox. Maybe a rainstorm last month, it looks like it has been sitting there so long. I hardly ever get anything in the mail other than ads for Sweet'N Low or from politicians who like to think they know me or flyers for donating to somewhere like downtown Baltimore, Where Hope Has Run Out. *Up in the corner, it shows that the letter is from the kid-glove guy, the broker. What mailing list of his would I be on? I'm going to rip the letter up and drop it to Sport's floor, where it can suck up the damp from my shoes. Then I think about how much I like to tear envelopes across the side. I rip it open just for the fun of it.*

The next day I bring what's inside to the bank. They say I have to show ID *if I want them to take me seriously. They have known me for more than thirty years, practically since I was born, but I am still pretty dirty from the grave digging. I go back to Sport and find my license in the glove box—at least those creeps didn't take that—and by the time I return, even the lady who is the receptionist is nice. But no matter. They say they need two extra days for it to clear.*

It turns out he did play his hunches after all. Mr. Kid Gloves wrote in the letter that I was the one to benefit, that it just took a long time to reach me because banks like to hold on to people's money for as many days as they can. And here it is—you're the survivor.

I'll take the first three zeroes in cash, I say, and I park Sport at the motel and ask for a room for myself. Although I have worked there for four years at least, I have to give them all that cash in advance so they won't have to drag me out of the room when the cops come to take me to the poorhouse, because how else will this end?

I cry and I cry. This time I am grateful.

45

After all that digging, I skip the next day entirely. Although I am at work, I only sit by the phone, expecting any moment to confess. It is not a busy season, and few people will call about grain and distract me. I rub liniment into my blistered hands, making picking up the phone tricky. When a patrol car drives into the lot, I first wonder whether they would be lenient if I rushed out and confessed, but that considering takes about the same amount of time as it does for the car to turn around and go back down the highway after someone. This cop was just using the driveway as a turnaround. I switch on the phone's answering device. I don't want to hear *Please come down and answer a few questions about a lot of dead sod and loose dirt and your fingerprints on a shovel.* Because we probably left the big shovel behind. I can't remember if Aphra took it—nothing's very clear about what went on while we made our frantic exit, and then faced the burned boys.

I do have these blisters. I consider wearing gloves and telling everyone—if anyone wants to know—that I've been out in the yard, gardening too much. But it's almost dead winter, and nobody digs now if they don't absolutely have to. At lunch I buy bulbs and empty the bag beside the office door, throwing a few down and digging them in wherever, wincing, wincing, wincing. I make their placement around the trailer look natural, as if they just grew here by accident. It was an accident, I will tell the officer. I was in a digging mood and thought, *Where else would nobody mind?*

Who is more guilty? A woman who pretends her brother is dead all his life and then wants to dig him up, resurrect him so she can make it up to him? Or the woman who kissed him but didn't save him, who wants him still, dead or alive? Or the burned Shove-It boys, the Hoods who harassed him all his adult life, who could be continuing their harassment?

While I wait by the phone all day, unable to do any work or even think, I read from the kind of book that doesn't require staring-out-the-window thinking but replaces all thought with Olympic swimming pools of savage love and intrigue written out on billboard paragraphs you can't help but decipher a page ahead and then turn that page. Finally, it occurs to me, reading so much about plot, that a cop who is the father of one of the boys could, if he wanted, find a way not to look too closely into the cemetery situation and the boys robbing us.

By the time I get home, all those hours later, I've decided the police won't call—they'll just come over and clap cuffs on my wrists. I might as well relax. My mother, staggering into the kitchen with a hangover, says my hands look terrible. Even an idiot uses hand lotion this season.

I spend a lot of time that night cooking family favorites and stay beside the stove with my hands inside pot holders. Did you hear that somebody tried to dig up your brother's grave? says my son first thing.

Really? I say. Sounds like a lot of trouble. I stir the pot.

My father says, The medical school in Lincoln must need another body. They don't like to publicize it, but somebody with that kind of radioactivity would be pretty interesting.

Radioactivity? says my son, accepting his filled plate from me.

Maybe the aliens did it, I say.

My father says, You think I'm nuts, don't you? That's one thing about your mother, he says, frowning at his plate. She always sees the kernel of truth, and that's all a farmer needs to plant. He lets me pile on double slices and scoops of everything. Radioactivity explains it pretty well, I'd say.

Only he and I know about the uranium handling. My son just shrugs.

I'm wondering how to eat from my own plate wearing the pot holders, selecting each potato wedge with much gravity, when my mother takes it upon herself to rise from the divan in the next room and enter. How long are you staying? she asks me.

She must have been talking to my father. If the elevator doesn't work out long term, I say, turning away from my half-filled plate, I could take over Dad's books, help with the bank, watch the markets.

My father eyes me. My brother must have seen this cold look of his and paused. You think I'm getting old? he says, in accusation.

I think farming's a big job.

My father chews and swallows and spears and then jabs his fork at me. What do you know about it?

I am a quick learner, I want to say, but that line's best when you're in fourth grade and there's new math to master. I say, I've spent months and months at the elevator.

My mother just smiles and heads back to her divan.

The next day, I buy six Healthy Choice selections, no one's favorites, and reconsider my resume, though when the man with the nice neck leaves a message about art later that afternoon, I return his call.

46

Shakespeare had a lot of plots. While I'm waiting for the rest of my money, I read through the whole book again, sitting inside Sport because the motel chair is a joke. If money go before, all ways do lie open. *I read not just the poetry and the donkey parts but pages I don't think anyone would read without a glass of water and a Tylenol. So many of those plots end up in death. Like he or she eats hot coals or gets torn apart by people who hate poets, or poisoned or hanged. Or else both arms and legs get whacked off, or people beheaded or buried up to the neck and starved. They get into lots of sword fights, and some even fall on their swords, which seems pretty stupid. They get chased by hungry bears, people get drowned, some commit suicide but with help, not to mention all those girls dying of broken hearts. He kills as many people as in the Bond movies. You'd think it was hard for him to end a play any other way.*

I dwell—I like that word, dwell*—on the ones with a broken heart as the problem. It's like china that falls to the floor—the pieces are everywhere, reflecting sadness whenever the light hits them. But with blood all around.*

Or else kissing.

With two hundred thousand actual dollars, what could I do? My teachers in high school always said more school is the best idea, but I am suspicious, because that's what they like. I could buy more clothes, except that clothes change styles all the time and it is not so worth it in my size. Fancy food like bib lettuce, which sounds to me like something you could wear, or beets all chopped up with cheese cubes? Maybe I should move somewhere that has a cook. I could give a chunk of the money to my mom like she said she wants so she could take some time off and not have to hope my dad gets a job.

I don't think so.

47

My mother is on the way to the freezer with glass in hand, diminishing the number of trips she will have to make in toto forever, and I am looking in her desk drawer for the keys to my brother's house for a final clean-out before the realtor gets there. She has made a few trips to the freezer for ice already today, back and forth. This time she stops en route and catches me at her desk, where she increases in size from someone you're not sure is breathing to someone who could find another bottle in a snowstorm, and she plucks those keys I want from their drawer. Did you know they clamped my legs together and that's why?

I hold out my hand for the keys. Clamped?

When your brother was coming through the canal. She sings this at the end, with "Coming through the Rye" as the tune. She doesn't give me the keys. She walks to the closet, which is now fully resupplied, and she finds what she needs for her ice. It's a big bottle that's hard to open with the keys in one hand. She puts the keys down to struggle with the cap. They had to have a doctor in attendance then, she says. Not your husband beside you like they do now.

I couldn't get my husband through the door when I was delivering, I say. Wild horses, I say. It was a sure sign he wasn't going to work out.

You were never very patient, she says.

I'll take those, I say, pointing at the keys beside her.

She's so wound up in her story, she doesn't hear me. You had to have a doctor to deliver then, like you needed a medical witness, she says. It's the way the nurses in Chicago have to be around when you're undressing, to see if you've got anything concealed.

I thought they did that to make sure you didn't fall down.

She laughs. The keys clink together on her fingers. The doctor was late, she says, after I palm them.

She gets the bottle unscrewed and pours herself another big one. Don't you see? They clamped my legs together because they had to wait for the doctor. Your brother was never the same.

How do you know he was never the same? Never the same as what? He was a fetus before—you didn't know him.

You don't get enough air in there, she says, screwing the cap back on and returning the bottle—still heavy enough—to the cupboard, you don't get enough air to the brain in time and it's all finished. It's no use after. You get seizures.

She takes a sip of scotch off the top of her ice, which starts cracking in little fissures.

I slip my brother's keys into my pocket. I'll be back in an hour or so.

He should've waited, she says. I was doing my best. I screamed. She gives an example.

I believe you, I say.

What part do you believe? she asks, stirring the drink with a meat thermometer, the first thing she finds in a drawer. What part don't you want to hear?

I'm not a child any more

Pity, she says. You were wonderful as a child.

The key has to be wiggled, and then the lock sticks. I squirt it with some WD-40 I have brought along, and I wiggle the key again. The door opens to the smell of a rotting house, the way newspaper gets if it's inside plastic too long in the sun. I pry open the windows for the realtor, I move the chairs around in my brother's front room so they face each other, as if people have come to talk, as if I could.

I am the mother of my brother because my mother wasn't a mother to me, so maternally I feel responsible for his dying, a mother who mourns the loss of even baby chicks and other people's infants because she's never going to be vigilant enough, because she'll never make the grade. A mother's not supposed to let anything die. Each death means there will be fewer offspring—not more to divide for those left, the way the greedy see it.

This is a viewpoint that the man with the nice neck does not get. I don't have to go very far into explaining myself when I discover this. He is very small-town inside those blue eyes of his, I am surprised to find out. I am almost grateful to discover something new, even that, in this small town. But what did I expect? He actually moved here instead of away—he wants to live here. I don't tell him anything about my investigation, but that doesn't matter. He has heard about the dog. It doesn't take but two evenings perched on the edge of chairs just about this far away to find out how limited his views are. Not that we talk about my brother. I kiss him anyway, goodbye.

Then gossip reaches me, even me, that Aphra's rich because of my brother. Surely she'll leave us alone at last. *Nothing can come of nothing*, she wrote on our fence last week. I thought she used one of those graffiti felt-tips, but it turned out to be the stuff they put on nails and came right off with a little turpentine.

I thought we had her for a minute, on a misdemeanor at the very least.

48

My mom invites me for the holiday, and I know from my mom that seconds are not involved, no gravy, only more salt. Leave your money at the door *is her real reason for the invitation. Everybody in town knows what I have, because that is the way it is when money goes through the bank. I come to dinner anyway, having nowhere else to go, as long as Mom promises I don't have to sit next to my dad. He scares me when he answers the door, so shaky-looking and polite in his khakis and white polo shirt. Hello, he says, like I am someone he has just met.*

I can't talk. I just nod and go right past him.

So many people come to dinner from my mother's hello-goodbye jobs: the lawn mower man, the gas station cashier, two motel maids, the sad kid who kills at the animal shelter, the cleanup person at the hospital who can hardly walk. They are all dressed up. They smile at me and my good fortune, telling each other and me what a great world they live in, thank the lord, anything can happen. That's my mom too, and she thanks me as if she has never thrown me out. Or is that something she's giving thanks for too?

I don't ask for butter to put on top of my turkey.

The old man who pushes the mower, who can hardly hold a spoon and has warts all over his face, says to me how much he loves this town, every single doggone blade of grass he mows all summer, the way it comes up and grows, giving him a living.

Maybe this town isn't so bad? Where else is the person who hugs a blind, deaf dog so hard it squeals the same person who puts him down ten minutes later? This kid—too young to be one of the ones who dumped fill into a front yard and got burnt—this kid has a job that makes him both hard and soft. He's in a foster home, or at least I think that's what it is. His parents went somewhere this weekend to pick up more kids, and how could they do that unless they're doing it for a living? My mother gives him a beer even if he's not old enough. Too many calories for me, I know.

They think the money will fix everything.

49

Spontaneous combustion, says my father, is what started creation. He makes this remark while we are filing in to our turkey dinner like firemen carrying a length of hose, which we should be. Since my mother doesn't eat with us, she doesn't cook, but whatever I cook from scratch often catches fire. On Sundays, I am worse about cooking with smoke than my father is with his backyard of smokers, and even more so on Thanksgiving. It's a family tradition, my burnt offerings. Always when the bird is out or has slipped to the floor in a greasy schmear with a fork stuck in its breast but not yet a knife, something else burns. It could be brussels sprouts left a little too long or bread put under the broiler. Last year, the relish burst into flame, my brother swore afterward, whose silence we miss—a parenthesis of discomfort as familiar as the gray haze we eat by that no one even notes anymore, other than a brief struggle over the less charred of the potatoes.

Our mother isn't one of the strugglers. She drinks and eats chocolates on that divan a room over. Chocolates provide lots of vitamins, she tells us when we try to coax her to dinner, and she just takes another. Especially good for you at Thanksgiving, she says. The Pilgrims would have had chocolate a few years later. The Indians went south like anybody sensible, to warm places that grew chocolate, where people ground it or ate it or tucked it into little mounds you could take north. South is where it's at, she says, not here with the mashed turnips at Thanksgiving.

Mashed turnips are not her favorite.

She does attend the blessing, that moment of steam. My son does the honors, does the best he can to think of ways we are thankful, in that voice that is turning into my brother's more every day. My mother then separates herself from the plate passing, with a new clatter of cubes, and her own drink freshening. By dessert—ours, not hers—she is prone again on her divan, eyeing us from afar if we enter, as if we were leftovers in advance, people to be foiled and cold-shelved.

My singeing and flaming over, I am scraping off ruined bits from the piebald pots and smoldering dishcloths when my father notices my mother gone. He'd been watching football, requisite of the holiday, and didn't hear her shuffled going-out. I tell him I offered my son's services as chauffeur but she wouldn't hear of it, insulted by the idea that she needed someone to drive her to the package store. Did I think she was tipsy? I told her it was a holiday, so the store wouldn't be open. This is what a holiday is for, she said.

When the phone rings that first day afterward, my father waves his hand from his chair in an *Okay, you get it*.

Who me? my son mimes, while it goes on ringing, but of course, I answer it.

Where are you? I ask.

Wrong number, says the voice.

Let's not answer next time, I say. Let's let her stew.

My father's got his head in his V-ed hands, like a choice morsel being offered up. He is thinking: What can he do to woo her back? He used to bring home a dozen roses wrapped in tissue every time she miscarried.

Maybe we are what she has flown from this time. The whole role.

On the second day she is gone, we wonder how much gas she had, as if that is a determining factor since she would never fill the tank herself, until my son points out that she could have ditched the car in Denver and taken a plane to Paris.

She could've gone to the bank for more scotch money, I say, scrubbing a pot newly burned. Maybe she's thrown herself facedown on the bank's early poinsettias and eaten them.

Why do they plant those flowers, when they know they're poisonous? my father says, instead of *Don't talk smart.* He's worried.

He doesn't know where to look, other than the bank or the divan, other than Chicago or the Sip and Sizzle Liquor Store. It is so unlike her to have moved so far away from the aforementioned, but so like her to express herself in action. She was just saying how her son must have gone somewhere—what about south? says my father, looking at his watch. People look at their watches when there's nothing else.

She could have driven too fast and be dead, and that's why she hasn't called again, says my son.

We all look into middle distance where TV static forms. What about an ad in the back of the newspaper? A poster on a pole? I ask.

She never slows down, says my father.

Three days gone, my father says not to call the police. She'll call again. Definitely.

She has never run away before, so where does he get this information?

The next day, my father goes so far as to get a haircut and buy roses.

The phone does ring again. We are sitting down to a surprisingly smoke-free spaghetti dinner, half-relaxed, or feigning it, so just anyone answers. *It's for you* is just as casual, and we lean toward each other instead of my father so as not to seem anymore interested than anyone else. We nod, my son and I, with our slight dissembling.

Put me on speakerphone, she tells my father. I have a message.

I am not hiding out, she says in that hollow way speakers have, but I will not tell you where I am. She talks about the weather in Florida, the trouble she had getting a rent-a-car in Tampa, her room key number. The phone machine interrupts to ask for another quarter. The truth is, she says as she fumbles long-distance for her quarter instead of telling us her phone number—the truth is I can never remember where I am, the Hotel Del Mar or the Del Mar Ray or the Sands or the House of Pancakes. It's a guesthouse, I think, and now I've dropped my room key where this phone-on-a-stick ends, down some grate. But I don't think the room key had the name of the hotel on it anyway, she adds with her quarter. The room key had an Indian's head on it. I'm quite sure of that.

No one asks why she fled so suddenly at Thanksgiving. No one knows what to say.

A big truck passes her phone.

Mom, I say, Tampa is a large city. Where would you stay if Dad were to come and get you?

You know, your brother was smarter than you. We had him tested, she says. He's not here, by the way. I've called the number he gave me a hundred times, and all I get is some man who doesn't even sound like a man who finally asked me if I would I give my son his name so he could give him a free massage. I said no, certainly not.

She starts to cry.

Stay where you are, says my father.

I'll just sit right down here, she says and cries louder. You can almost hear her slide down the phone support.

We let her sit since the connection quits and we have no number. My mother is not a cell phone adopter. My father flies to Tampa and follows the spoor of her credit card to a nice place where you could spend your honeymoon, as she puts it to him after he's tipped everyone like a gentleman, as if he's someone she would consider.

A lot of ashtrays come back in her bag. My son says we should start smoking and get some use out of them. They provide places for snacks, I say, food you could eat at a family dinner instead of what burns, food that a family like this could choke on.

50

It takes me awhile to search online at the library to figure out what exactly the bait should be. Then it has to be sent somewhere, since I can't trust that Mom won't look in the mailbox. I have to rent a box for a week that I cancel as soon as it comes. I don't want someone to know I have it.

It's like I have a life starting but I keep having to cancel it.

Soon.

I lock the door to the motel room twice. The bolt too. I undress myself completely and take a long time in the bathtub. I make it hotter and hotter. I pretend it is the hot tub we enjoyed so much together before our fresh dessert.

51

Buyers for my brother's house are a breed of people my father says are rare after a sudden death. Two old people from a big city who don't know—Where does it say you have to say?—saw the ad, with its price so low they couldn't put the paper down until they called us. They want a place to park themselves during the summer, they say. Not too big. With the fields nearby.

Okay.

Inside my brother's fridge sits a covered bowl of green Jell-O. A double-thick batch with only one scoop taken out. Its green irregular edges quiver pristinely when I touch it, lively under its sterile plastic, as if it hasn't been sitting in this fridge for, lo! these many months since my brother made it.

I put it outside for a stray.

That is hard for me. I want the Jell-O to show his spoon marks forever, I want to stand at the door with its filthy windows uncleaned for that long, and I want to see exactly what he saw. But already the huge mound of fill from the Shove-It boys, the burned ones, the Hoods, has settled into a new landscape of snowy dips and rolls and dead weeds. The moles or prairie dogs and the neighbors' kids, with their cardboard sleds, are helping with these rolls, so much so that it looks landscaped. Over there a tree has fallen down in a neighbor's yard—a different view, surely, from my brother's. And whose dog is this that comes slinking around for the Jell-O? No one's I know.

Inside, I fling open cupboards. The kitchen in this garage of a house is built like a ship, rocket or not, with a hatch and a door for everything. Behind one with a squarish knob, I find three dozen more boxes of Jell-O.

My brother had taste. All-lime taste. Boxes on boxes of lime Jell-O. I take out the first row, stacked close like a supermarket's, and then there's another. How did the auction people miss this?

I select one box and shift the contents, listening to its sweet powder move from one cardboard side to the other. I rip open the cardboard and then the paper sack and tongue its green, its completely convincing sweet green taste.

Three dozen boxes of green Jell-O. A naked man. A three-hundred-pound woman. A hot tub. I review each as I toss box after box into a black trash bag. I try to think Jell-O, like him.

He had drawings for the Jell-O cushion and airbag. He had the okay from the Jell-O people, who say okay to almost anything that makes people buy more Jell-O. He tested his invention with a dummy and once had Aphra smash into one, and it worked fine. The barrier between the instant heat and the instant ice broke together like two-part epoxy, broke and mixed and set the Jell-O almost instantly. It was not unlike hitting a wall of foam.

He wanted ads on the back of the boxes, and that's where the Jell-O people drew the line. He sent samples to sports car makers, to drivers who raced in the Indie 500. He offered free cushions to people at Rotary car washes, even free installation. He stopped telling people what was inside. He said that it was a brand-new kind of cushion, patent pending, and that the reason why it was cheap was to gain acceptance. Then he raised the price to counter the taint of cheapness, to suggest that this was top-of-the-line, that you couldn't do better.

He needed the Jell-O for new experiments, for stock.

I empty the rest of the box I tasted out the door. Its powder flies away in the wind, off the porch, spraying a patch of snow with the color of green urine. Although it might worry my father with his alien ideas, the strays will like it.

The old dog that cleaned the bowl I set out is still hanging around, but it doesn't run over and sniff at the blown Jell-O or lick it. This dog turns his head way around to look close at the snow behind him, and then he starts howling. This howl isn't the one I keep hearing, especially when I don't want to, or even the one I heard on that day with the dog and his tail. This one is not a dog-with-a-burn howl. This one makes a lost howl, not focused on fire or a moon or a girl dog's hind end. This dog walks four steps with his four legs and falls over, then scrambles up and walks again, howling, and falls again. Halfway across the yard, he gets the hang of walking and howling together and turns around and wags at me.

I have done nothing to receive such a wag, other than put out the bowl. In fact, I close the door on the dog as it howls again at the far end of the yard, as that howl goes a little gleeful.

Must have been great Jell-O. Must have had something in it, but I'd have to kill the dog to find out what.

I bring the bowl back in and wash its licked-clean insides, overturn it on the rack, and then quickly dry it with a towel. Then I double-bag the rest of the Jell-O.

It's another something of him I want to keep, more of the mystery of his death, the singed military discharge, the syringe that sits in my desk drawer with its exclamation of a red herring, of a whole school of fish that is not so easily found.

Locking up, I see that the ring where the hot tub sat is less snowy than anywhere else. I imagine my brother and Aphra sitting in the tub with icicles on their noses, so intimate with each other after all their driving together, the hot steam fogging their faces. Inside on the table there could have been a big bowl of green Jell-O, an aphrodisiac so sweet it's almost cough medicine flavor, with only half the water in it, thick and green, left cooling on the table in the low-temp house my brother always had, while two people steam-soaked outside. Just the kind of treat those fresh out of a hot tub could eat in a frisky way.

52

I look in Sport's mirror a lot these days, to be sure I'm really here—the strangeness of being so alone doesn't ever wear off, despite having money and people with ideas about how to spend it. And now there are wrinkles around my eyes, along with the sadness.

I may be in neutral, but I got the bait ready.

53

It went like this, my son tells me in a scared voice. It happened just a couple of hours ago, not like it was dark or anything. I was waiting for you to pick me up at the skate park.

Sorry, I couldn't find my keys. And then the phone rang, and I got into something. Then I forgot you. You should have called again.

I was out of power. He sighs big and heavy. Pulling his legs up under his chin, he looks twelve instead of sixteen, a little kid all alone in the middle of his bed. Listen to me.

I'm listening.

I was just standing there, he says. Some guys drove off—we were joking around—and she pulled in right where they were. She didn't open her door. She rolled down her window and held out a box that she had inside her car. Here, she says. It was *Hell in Traffic*, aka HIT. Everybody wants it, even the jocks. Really great graphics. But I didn't grab it. I said, Nice. She said, I'm sorry—I'm really sorry for making trouble for all of you. This is for you.

I pat his foot next to where I'm sitting at the edge of his bed.

Really, Mom—she said that.

She has her good points, I'm sure.

But she didn't give me the box, she was, like, wiggling it in her hand. Just let me talk to you a little while, she said. I have something else I have to say.

He draws circles with his fingers on his bedspread.

You didn't.

Hey, he says. I told her I don't take candy from just any stranger.

But he doesn't make that sound so funny.

Go on, I say.

So I take the box and open it. It was all in there. Brand-new. Thanks, I said to her. Then she says she wants to take me somewhere to talk so nobody will see her with me. That sounded okay with me. I didn't want to be seen talking to her, and I mean, she's sorry, right? I got in, and she drove so slowly out of the place, I could have jumped out like they do in the movies.

I hope not.

He brushes the hair out of his eyes the way my brother used to. But she wasn't talking, at least not then.

His voice goes soft there, as if he can't find his own words.

And?

Are you going to burn me like those boys? is what I asked her. It just popped into my head—me in the hot seat, not knowing where we were going. You know, everybody thinks she burned those boys now that they know you didn't.

Geez, I say, doesn't anybody believe that the boys did it to themselves?

My son shrugs as if that is too much to ask.

So—what is it she wanted to tell you?

She parked next to the emergency room at the hospital, the side entrance. It was a weird place. Like, am I going to need a doctor?

Yeah, I say, not good.

After I asked her about the burning, she said she had just bought drugs from those guys—you were right about that—and then they jumped her. Their dads did it is how they put it, so they would too, and then after that, they started chasing the dog.

All this comes out in a rush.

Oh, I say. That's terrible.

She's pretty strong, but I guess three of them were too many.

He throws himself to the carpet in a twist of nervousness. I heard the bells ring at the church about that time. Nothing bad was going to happen to me if I could hear them is what I thought.

At least they're good for something, I say.

Go on, I say, since he's stopped talking again.

I didn't do anything to you is what I said. I like the game, I said. Thank you—I said thank-you twice. She got all worked up. She could have left those boys when they were so burned and screaming, she said. She could have dumped them on the way to the hospital.

He stops for so long, I ask if that's all. I whisper it—I'm filled with fear.

He swallows some air. She turned around and leaned over the seat and grabbed both sides of my head. When I tried to get away, she gave me what I think is the longest mouth-to-mouth kiss ever made by a human, past and future.

I make a little sound. Oh.

When I finally got her off me, all she said was she thought it was her kiss that killed him.

My brother?

That was what the hospital was for. I had to find out, she said, if that was the problem.

So, he says, I took the game—I earned it—and I got out right then and there and started walking home. On the way, it was really cold, and I had a long time to think about being dead. But here I am.

I hug him and hug him.

Kidnap and abuse are what I tell the officer.

Kinky is what the officer tells me. A woman like that. A young boy. I know about the restraining order, he sighs. It's still in effect. Have him come into the office in the morning to fill out a complaint.

While my father calls the lawyer who wrote up that order, I go into my son's room.

Go away, says my son, talking to the wall. It was my business, and now everybody's going to know.

I had to.

You didn't have to do anything.

I look down at his long limbs wrapped around the chair. Aren't you worried she'll do it again? She needs help.

I don't think she will, he says. She's finished. She said she got what she wanted.

54

Get thee to a nunnery, said the girl's boyfriend in Shakespeare, when he meant brothel. She thought he was crazy—that was her mistake.

First you put in hot, then you put in ice cubes.

55

Aphra is sighted floating down the river on an inner tube in ice fishermen's gear with hay in her hair. My son tells me this in the garage, just after I'm released from his last practice drive.

I can't imagine her floating, I say.

My son says it's physics. It's possible.

I hang up my coat on the hook inside the door. The river must be pretty cold this time of year.

Very, says my son. Weird, he says. She is fine, though. That's what the guy at the gas station said.

Rape survivors often can't feel cold, or else they feel it all the time. But I don't tell him this. I say, What's for dinner? It's your turn.

Maybe she enjoyed it, he says. My friends—he says, opening the fridge—we've been spying on her. I think she put a knife in one of the burned boy's tires.

Did they accuse her? Those boys have dads in law enforcement, I know.

I think they're going to lock her up. He skates around on the ottoman, consulting his phone.

How about pickles and cheese for dinner?

Let's try steak tartare, he says. Online it says you just thaw hamburger and serve it. That's even easier than microwaving.

Ha. I put an onion on the table. You have to cut this up to go with it.

I look over at my son, texting a new friend, *some girl.*

Aphra dealt him nothing cruel in the end, not really, just a kiss. But it's never the end, in a small town. I have to make a decision, and she is still part of it. I consider his six reasons why he can't mow the lawn in the summer, starting with allergies like my brother, and my son's disinterest in even a bean sprouting in a paper cup in kindergarten. Did you ever want to be a farmer? I ask him as soon as he puts down his phone. Now that you know something about it.

He rolls his eyes.

I prepare our last box of green Jell-O. I have put the rest of it in cakes, in permanents, in tea for nail strength, between ladyfingers and wafers, and around celery, pineapples, and walnuts. None of it has made us fall down like the dog. My son and I eat a plate of it first, straight up and cold, as a kind of appetizer—not that it works that way.

To celebrate finishing the lime Jell-O, we play a game I've devised. Jell-O is the modus operandi. My son gets the first turn and guesses that the murderers use Jell-O frozen into points and dipped in venom. One hit, he says, and it melted inside him, and then there's no evidence.

But there's always a mark, I say. A place where the point goes in.

You've got a point there, says my son, without the least pun remorse.

You could throw a block of Jell-O from an airplane at fifty thousand feet, I say. It would freeze solid on the way down and then, bang, hit him on the head when he's walking in from the tub. Then the Jell-O melts, and there's no evidence at all.

Except for the concussion, says my son. Same as the one you get when you toss Jell-O out the door from a failed experiment and then you slip on it, frozen, getting out of the hot tub.

We're both quiet. Then my son bursts out, LSD in the Jell-O! He eats it first from the bowl, and instead of having her share of the drug, she kisses him. Then his heart stops.

Maybe, I say.

The kiss! The kiss! My son gives his Jell-O a big one. Is the sound of his smack the one we heard at the séance? Or does it recall the one he survived with Aphra? My son looks stricken by my second question, but then his look seems more to be about some text that's dinged on his cell phone than the sound he's made. And then he says, LSD doesn't leave any trace in the blood. He's just researched it.

I get up and wash out the rim of the last rubbery bits that stick to a bowl after you finish all but one helping, my father's, set out on a plate. These bits dissolve down the drain the way they always do, the way they did after I brought in my brother's old Jell-O bowl, after that strange dog licked it, howled, and fell down—this very same bowl.

Or you could choke on the Jell-O, my son goes on, flicking his phone off. Make it super thick like that Japanese kind of food. They could have been passing it mouth-to-mouth in another sort of weird kiss, and it caught in his throat and choked him. It could have melted later.

Right. Or she could have poured it hot into his ear, I say. Only, she loved him. I swirl more water around in the bowl.

The front door opens, and there's the sound of my father taking off his work boots—two thumps.

He comes in late to eat ever since my mother took the train to Chicago again, where someone she met helped her out of her seat and into a cab that took her to what we are now calling her second home. Maybe he comes late because he can pretend she is just in the other room, sorting her assorted chocolates. Maybe he comes late because he knows I am looking for work, but not here.

He bears a smoked leg of lamb, his first try. Ham-lamb, he calls it. I thought it would go well with the Jell-O, he says, as he sits down to his wavery last portion. We can pretend it's mint jelly.

We sure need something else. All I have is hamburger and this. I point at the onion.

Go to the grocery store, says my father. It won't kill you.

I make a face.

Do they cough at the end? my son asks me while I find a knife for the smoky meat.

Does who cough at the end? my father says. Oh, he says, looking down at his plate as if my brother's bones are ground up in the Jell-O. This is the last box, isn't it?

Geez, says my son. The last. He mimes an IV feeding, one arm up in the air. The drip, the drip! That's all that's left.

Even though you sound like my brother now, I say, the longer he's dead, the less you're like him. There's no mirror at the bottom of the hole.

My family chooses not to ask me what I mean by that hole.

I heard they arrested one of the burned boys today, says my father, opening his napkin. He was caught stealing school trophies.

My son nods. It happened in shop.

Young kids know the value of silver plate? I'm surprised, I say.

They found drugs inside it, says my son. Maybe it was the LSD I made up, he says.

Maybe the cops were always in on it, I say.

My father chuckles with his disbelief.

There was this bowl in the fridge, I say. There was one bite taken out, I say. And the dog did howl after licking it. Howled strange and long and stumbled. I think I told you about it. It could have been LSD.

Windowpane, says my son.

Stop it, my father says. He says, Stop it again and then offers each of us a slice of lamb. I don't want to hear any more about this again ever. It's enough. Epileptics can't take extreme changes of temperature, but I told the county coroner I didn't want *seizure* on the certificate, and he obliged.

We look at our plates piled with meat. We pick up forks and knives.

Remember the lawn mower man? my father asks me while he saws at his meat. The one who has warts all over his face?

Yes, I say. Want some of the peas I found in the freezer? I can microwave them.

Thank you, he says. Those warts were from the war he went to—some chemical made them. They weren't from kissing little girls like I said. Well, he just died.

All this bad kissing, says my son.

No, Dad, really? I say. All those years when I thought you thought he was after me. It was a kind of chemical poisoning that killed him?

Maybe what killed your brother was completely different from what it looks like, he says, looking at his plate.

You mean, we'll never know the truth, I say, handing around the hot peas.

It cost me plenty to fix the sprinklers at the cemetery, he says. They sent me a bill.

I don't look him in the eye, which is guilt enough.

I hear they keep the cemetery locked at night now, my son says. Nobody can get in—or out. He giggles.

Quiet, says my father.

It's only three o'clock when we finish. The sun is not setting, because this is Sunday dinner in medias res, finished just in time for naps or play or cards.

I deal out cards for pitch. My father wins the kitchen silver and my son's new CD and half the cash in my wallet. My son wins my father's brand-new double smokers, his turn at dishes, and the golf ball I found outside his room. Then I win, and I keep the syringe, the last empty box of Jell-O, and the sound of my brother's bell.

56

Take care of Aphra is what I tell Aphra that my brother was trying to say in all his appearances—at the séance, in the wall molding, and the dust storm. Of course she thinks I'm the one who's crazy. She's the expert, recovering from her own crazy, from her voyage down the river to the rest home, the only place in this town they put people if they break down physically or mentally. At least it's not the motel my brother lay in, day after day. She is watching the aviary they have there, finches and what look to me like wandered-in sparrows, singing and stealing seed from each other, but she's listening. I hand her the little shoebox of the rest of his things: the receipts and coupons, the Vegas tickets, his discharge, and we talk about birds.

The next time I come, she has a job feeding the birds and her fellow patients, as well as tidying—something to do, even if she has money. *'Tis in my memory lock'd, / And you yourself shall keep the key of it*, she says to me when I leave. I figure she's crazier than ever, and I ask my son, who might have studied something with a *'Tis* in it. He says, Give me a break.

Nonetheless, Aphra and I drive to the cemetery in the early spring, each in her own car. Aphra's looks more lived in than ever, but with a fancy curtain on one window. Why doesn't she buy a new one? She says she's comfortable with what she has. We leave a bouquet beside his stone, which I had engraved *Peace on Earth*, to match the sign he liked on his property. The sod already shows a little green. She looks over at me to check to see if my face is sad enough, and I guess it is, because she touches the lumpy sod with the toe of her shoe and says, You never asked me what happened.

I read the coroner's report, and I guessed—that was all. I'm stupid, I say, not to ask. I was afraid you'd get upset. Maybe I didn't want to know.

You were too sad.

What happened? I ask in a sad voice, as if she is right.

Wind catches at the scarf she wears usually to church, making her pull it tight around her face, which is a bit thinner after all that time working at the home. The blue in the scarf shows off her eyes that are not tucked so deep into her cheeks anymore. Well, she says, shaking her head the way you do when you're going solemn, we sat in his hot tub and got good and hot. Then we ran through the cold, back into his place. We did it two times. He said it was like the Jell-O—first the hot water, then the ice cubes. We were waiting for a whole big bowl of it to thicken up at least a little. We were doing the waiting back in the tub and were all toasty when I gave him a great big kiss, a pretty long one. Right then, he had a seizure, and I dragged him out, flopping and stiff and wild. I don't know how I did it. Then I had to drop him on the ground, because he was throwing himself all over. I ran inside to get the phone, but my hands were all wet, so I had to dry them off to call. I went into the bathroom to get a towel, and then I couldn't find the phone again, and then I remembered he had one of those with the cord. And 9-1-1 kept saying, What? like I was a crank, talking about the hot tub and all, but in the end, they took the address, but I left the phone off the hook I was so upset. Since he was still seizing up, I thought, *Good, I have time to get dressed*, and I pulled everything on and then got down on my knees and dragged him across the ground to the inside and put a blanket I ripped off the bed around him and held him tight, as best I could. I took one bite out of the Jell-O and tried to give it to him, but his teeth were shut tight so I ate it because I didn't know what else to do then. I held on to him, but he had gotten away by the time the ambulance finally came, and nobody could do nothing.

That's all there was to it?

Her look could boil water. It was terrible.

I'm sorry, I say.

She stomps on the ground around his plot, her whole weight on every footfall, to let him know that she told me. Sound carries through the ground, she says. Elephants talk to other elephants miles away by stomping—why not the living to the dead?

57

Two rockets about to take off is what we decide the grain elevators are, my father and I, driving his pickup home past them, with a full moon rising in between. We've come from an evening screening of one of those film-stunt sci-fi silent films delivered by the art car that my son refuses to enjoy, saying that if he can't hear any of the explosions, what good is it to go? We drive toward that meteor hole, which, we agree, is just a silent-film prop waiting for rockets and stunts and explosions. We could make our own sci-fi film, says my father. It would be cheap. A smart alien would not have tentacles or six legs or drool, he says. A smart alien would look like your son.

What about me? I say, as if neglected.

My father snorts.

I'm no longer alien. People now have coffee with me out of the boredom of a small town that passes for a kind of amnesia. They invite me to barbecues and get-togethers and don't ask how my mother is. If they did, I would tell them that she is coming home soon. The only lie I'd tell is where I say that she lost twenty pounds this time and looks healthier than ever, but of course, they know better anyway. She will pass the chocolates.

But I won't be here by then.

We are driving past that meteor hole when my father notices lights flickering from inside it. An alien landing? I ask.

My father lifts an eyebrow. Let's check.

I swerve off the road and drive the pickup—bump and crunch—over to the fence.

My son's car—the one he saved a little up for, then took a loan from me as soon as he knew we were moving to somewhere where he couldn't have a car—circles the meteor hole. Tracks around that hole show where the car has struggled for purchase, my son no doubt showing off this new car of his and his secret hole-in-the-ground by circling it in a contest of steering around and around. These tracks show gravity to be the winner, with the car near the bottom and getting closer to the bottom with every whine of its wheels.

We try not to get too upset, but it is clear we are not so sympathetic. The three boys we see inside have their hands pressed to the ceiling because my son is accelerating so fast, trying to get the car out of the hole, that they almost flip over. We laugh a little after they park at the bottom to tell us how it happened—we are that upset. Then my father backs around and hooks the two cars together with a cable I have long been trying to throw out of the trunk, then the boys and my son and my father holler and swear and pull and push, and someone produces a shovel.

Where did that come from? I ask, but they all get out and ignore me. They lever it under a wheel and tell me to drive. I drive the car forward whenever someone says, Now—I rock and I stop. In between, I look into the rearview mirror at this hole that they've fallen into, and I don't know what to make of it. Maybe it's a bull's-eye, a meteor's X-marks-the-spot, where anyone can land and break into countless pieces. Or it's an ant lion's den, a way to suck a not-so-innocent someone or thing into a circle to his doom. Or just a place to get burned up after you reenter, an electric charge branching and blooming, and then dust. A black hole with a shovel beside it under a big moon.

The pickup's at an angle, and in the windshield all I can see is the edge of the hole and the moon behind it. On that edge, in front of that moon, I make out—because what good is it to stare into the dark of the boys' problem?—about as alien a creature as you can think up. The shadow it makes could have been a fork and a knife and two moving oranges, so skinny the way it walks, down and then up, with the moon showing through bristle instead of fur. It could be a big cat, but a dog is possible, the way it passes along the edge at a lope, a burned, still-alive dog.

I look away. Then it's gone.

This is what it's like in the future, says my father, who comes to sit beside me in the car to say Now and to talk about anything other than my son's new car chagrin. The sun will be off, and there will be only a dark moon left, he says. Then a boy holds up his hand in a halt, and I brake. My father says, Now, and we go again. In the future, he says, it will be just like this, all cratered and dusty. This hole is what you get into when you get all cold, then stuff buries you or tries to. And in a million years, it's us here, or not us, a couple of cockroaches, says my father, giving the *Now* signal. Dead and gone, he says with the glee the old have about being closer to dead than anyone else.

My son and my son's friends finally heave the car out, and when they come around to get into the rescued car, I see my son is the one holding that shovel.

IN THE FLYOVER FICTION SERIES

Ordinary Genius
Thomas Fox Averill

Jackalope Dreams
Mary Clearman Blew

Ruby Dreams of Janis Joplin: A Novel
Mary Clearman Blew

Deer Season
Erin Flanagan

It's Not Going to Kill You, and Other Stories
Erin Flanagan

The Usual Mistakes, and Other Stories
Erin Flanagan

Reconsidering Happiness: A Novel
Sherrie Flick

Glory Days
Melissa Fraterrigo

Twelfth and Race
Eric Goodman

The Front
Journey Herbeck

The Floor of the Sky
Pamela Carter Joern

In Reach
Pamela Carter Joern

The Plain Sense of Things
Pamela Carter Joern

Toby's Last Resort
Pamela Carter Joern

Stolen Horses
Dan O'Brien

Haven's Wake
Ladette Randolph

Private Way: A Novel
Ladette Randolph

Because a Fire Was in My Head
Lynn Stegner

Bohemian Girl
Terese Svoboda

Dog on Fire
Terese Svoboda

Tin God
Terese Svoboda

Another Burning Kingdom
Robert Vivian

Lamb Bright Saviors
Robert Vivian

The Mover of Bones
Robert Vivian

Water and Abandon
Robert Vivian

The Sacred White Turkey
Frances Washburn

Skin
Kellie Wells

The Leave-Takers: A Novel
Steven Wingate

Of Fathers and Fire: A Novel
Steven Wingate

To order or obtain more information on these or other University of Nebraska Press titles, visit nebraskapress.unl.edu.

CPSIA information can be obtained
at www.ICGtesting.com
Printed in the USA
LVHW100549150223
739566LV00003B/422